THE BOOK OF DEATH

CONTENTS

Acknowledgements	ix
Author's Submission	xi
Preface	xiii
Chapter One	1
Chapter Two	9
Chapter Three	12
Chapter Four	17
Chapter Five	23
Chapter Six	30
Chapter Seven	34
Chapter Eight	37
Chapter Nine	44
Chapter Ten	49
Chapter Eleven	51

Chapter Twelve	57
Chapter Thirteen	61
Chapter Fourteen	65
Chapter Fifteen	69
Chapter Sixteen	76
Chapter Seventeen	86
Chapter Eighteen	88
Chapter Nineteen	97
Last Chapter	104

Dedicated to

the mysterious Sanskrit letter,

ऋ

and

the last chapter of this novel

ekadā

First published in Urdu as *Maut ki Kitab* in 2011 by Arshia Publications

Published in English as *The Book of Death* in 2025 by Ekadā, an imprint of Westland Books, a division of Nasadiya Technologies Private Limited

No. 269/2B, First Floor, 'Irai Arul', Vimalraj Street, Nethaji Nagar, Alapakkam Main Road, Maduravoyal, Chennai 600095

ISBN: 9789371979689

10 9 8 7 6 5 4 3 2

This is a work of fiction. Names, characters, organisations, places, events and incidents are either products of the author's imagination or used fictitiously.

Typeset by Jojy Philip

Printed at Thomson Press (India) Ltd

TRANSLATED FROM THE URDU BY

A. NASEEB KHAN

THE BOOK OF DEATH

KHALID JAWED

ekadā

ACKNOWLEDGEMENTS

I WISH TO PLACE ON RECORD MY HEARTFELT GRATITUDE to Professor Anisur Rahman, Professor M. Asaduddin and Ehteshamuddin Ahsan for their support and encouragement throughout the translation of this book. I am especially indebted to Professor Khalid Jawed, Mita Kapur, Founder and CEO of Siyahi, and Minakshi Thakur, Publisher at Westland Books. Their guidance and faith in this work have been invaluable. My sincere thanks must also go to Westland Books for graciously bringing this translation to print, lending it a wider audience and giving it its rightful place in the literary landscape.

A. Naseeb Khan
Jamia Millia Islamia
New Delhi

AUTHOR'S SUBMISSION

WITH UTMOST SINCERITY, I OFTEN ASK MYSELF THE question, 'Why do I write at all?' Writing and drawing scratches are almost the same thing. When we ponder the fundamental essence of the Sanskrit letter 'ऋ' (hri), it becomes even clearer. Drawing scratches on stones, clawing, rubbing and perpetrating cruelties on them – this is all that writing is. According to the fundamental spirit of the letter 'ऋ', writing is an act where no duality or distance exists between the author and his creation. The letter 'ऋ' is the sound of a fire burning – it incinerates all the impurities of writing. So, I am aware of my crime. Whatever I write is like drawing scratches on stones. I do not know whether the stones really feel pain or not, but my nails come off repeatedly. Writing is an excruciatingly painful act. Through writing, you inflict stinging pain on others, and moreover, a profound wound grows deep within you as well. Quite often, I have sincerely contemplated stopping the act of writing. However, the relentless flow of my poor humour and bad aesthetic taste seems never to end. Under the influence of some spectral presence, my nails dart repeatedly to etch lines on the stone. My readers, however, are at liberty to stop reading this book whenever they choose, not open it at all, or discard it entirely, consigning it to a drain. There is no fear of feeling any regret, or harbouring any malice in my heart due to their free will.

PREFACE

I CAME ACROSS THIS TEXT IN THE FORM OF A manuscript while wandering the ruins of Girgita Til Mas during my research exactly three years ago to determine whether two multinational companies could build a steel plant there. It has now been conclusively established that these are the ruins of a mental asylum. An international archaeological institute once sent a six-member team to this region in the Far East, where a small city named Girgita Til Mas existed about two hundred years ago. It was particularly renowned for a mental asylum, its large population of chameleons and sesame farming. The city was purposefully submerged in water for the construction of a hydroelectric dam by the central government. Before flooding this city, its inhabitants were relocated to another place.

However, due to the ecological imbalance on the planet over the past few years, all the rivers in the region either dried up or changed their courses. Mountainous terrain transformed into plains, and the power plant became as useless as a limb without function, so it was demolished. Two hundred years later, the city resurfaced with its ruins and debris. I found this manuscript among those ruins, placed within a fissure in a broken rock. Black in colour, it was a hardbound volume, squeezed between a mossy stone and wild shrubs and roots grown within the crack in the rock. This rock was certainly a part of the wall of that mental asylum. It is a matter of considerable surprise that despite being under water for two hundred years, the book was not at all damaged. None of its pages had dissolved in the water; even the binding was intact. God knows why the water hadn't affected it. Since I am interested in ancient manuscripts and scholarly texts, I retrieved it from the crevice, dusted it off and kept it safely in my possession. The manuscript was written in a strange language, each letter of which was unfamiliar and entirely unintelligible to me.

Our team stayed in Girgita Til Mas for ten days, completed the assigned work and returned thereafter. The report was subsequently submitted to the institute, indicating that the two multinational companies could now be permitted to found the world's largest steel unit on that land. We did not find anything or any building of significant archaeological value buried under the debris in Girgita Til Mas. As far as the ruins of the mental asylum are concerned, what historical importance could they possibly hold?

However, I couldn't take my attention away from this manuscript. When I carried out a thorough investigation into its language and the script used, I discovered that this tongue was read, written and spoken in this region and its surroundings two to three hundred years ago, but now it is practically impossible to find anyone who can understand it. Moreover, there is no library in the entire world where a book written in this language can be traced. The details of the writers of this language have long been erased from the internet, and nothing has been preserved in digital form either. The reasons for its extinction are not evidently clear. They may be attributed, to some extent, to national politics, the ill-fortune of this language, and the apathy and materialism of the community that once spoke and wrote in it. However, this is not the right time to delve into these details.

Finally, I sent this text to my friend Jean Hugo, whose ancestry traces back to the celebrated scholar and orientalist Garcin de Tassy. I had often heard Hugo mention that Garcin de Tassy had learnt a few Eastern languages and had conducted some noteworthy researches in their fields of study.

I received no response from Hugo for almost a year. I had nearly forgotten about the manuscript. But one day I received a letter from him, saying that he had successfully read almost the entire text. He mentioned that there were some program files of the script for this language on his computer, which he dug out after considerable effort. Hugo then sent me a machine translation of the manuscript.

I am now summoning the courage to present this translation to you. The manuscript does not bear the name of any author, nor does it offer any clues about who might have written it. I have neither added to nor subtracted anything from this text. However, at several places, numerous paragraphs were repeated without any logical coherence, as if the author had recurrently forgotten that he had already written them verbatim earlier. In view of the principles of research, I have not included the repeated paragraphs.

In addition to these issues, the text contains some spelling mistakes and errors related to the usage of masculine and feminine genders of words. Neither Hugo thought it proper to correct them in his translation, nor did I, as they might have been correct according to the rules of grammar of this language at the time. Another notable point is that the last pages of the book are blank. Nothing is written on them, but they have been numbered in an orderly manner, indicating that the author deliberately left them blank. But there is no clear indication of the book's conclusion, even though the text ends. I have, therefore, included these pages in their original form, following the core tenets of research. There were some sketches in the manuscript, which have also been retained as they were.

Now, I am publishing this book in the language that everyone in the world knows today. The objective of bringing out this book is solely to give the readers insights into the individual or collective issues, or the emotional lives of the people of that time. Otherwise, this book neither throws light on any historical aspects of Girgita Til Mas nor can it be regarded as a substantial work of literary merit. At best, it can be classified under Dutch writing, which refers to writing done in a state of intoxication.

I am deeply indebted to my friend Jean Hugo, to whom this work owes its existence. Without his tireless efforts and invaluable assistance, this book would never have seen the light of day, though he was against the publication of this book, considering it a futile work with no possibilities of any fruitful outcome.

1 April 2211

Professor Walter Schiller
Department of Archaeology
Seoukargifurt University, Seoukargifurt

CHAPTER ONE

SUCH NIGHTS OCCUR VERY RARELY – PERHAPS ONLY once in a span of fifteen to twenty years. Tonight is one such night when the distance between the moon and Earth is drastically reduced, and the moon's radiance is unusually intense. Overcome with panic, I am squatting here in the confines of the inner room. This condition of the moon is set to persist for approximately four hours – and these hours will weigh heavily on the world. The possibility of devastating storms and earthquakes looms large on the horizon. Silence reigns supreme within every household. Footfalls are heard not even in the street. Everyone is gripped by fear. Each engrossed in their own prayers. Even so, who is not aware of the injurious effects of the moonlight, such as discomfort, high blood pressure, depression, and an overwhelming impulse to commit suicide?

Squatting down on the floor always brings me a feeling of relaxation, or, as it seems, I have grown accustomed to it. When my kneecaps, calves and heels go numb, it's as if the Earth's gravitational pull gets defeated by them. Then I lose no opportunity of humiliating this void Earth.

In a corner of this dark room lies my mother's drum. Quite frequently, I feel the urge to beat it loudly. But in the next moment, I realise that the time for that act has not yet come. One should play a musical instrument only after being able to transform oneself into a melody, which I still can't. There is a ventilator in the rear wall of this room from where a corner of tonight's menacing moon is peeping in. The long tail of a chameleon remains stuck to the frame fixed around the ventilator. Behind the wall stretches a street, and from the left bend of that street runs another street which terminates in a dead end. A dry well stands over there. People keep dumping garbage and abandoned carcasses of stray dogs and cats in this well. These carcasses putrefy over there. Will tonight's menacing and furious moon revive the dead water source within this dry well? Will it acquaint the dark well, which is now brimming with waste, with the ebb and flow of tides? I have no idea. I am not at all scared of this night or this moon. I am not alone here. I have someone else with me. I am, in fact, terrified by a pointed white bone jabbing at my heart as I sit here. This has been troubling me for several days now. This bone seems to be piercing my heart. And from the evening until midnight, I have either been squatting within the confines of this house, or moving from one place to another, sometimes on the dilapidated steps of the staircase, sometimes in the mud-courtyard and sometimes inside my bedroom.

Outside this room, my father enjoys a deliciously peaceful sleep, snoring on the verandah, while in the adjoining room my wife will now be tossing and turning in her bed. But I am not alone here. I have someone else with me. It has been constantly following me since time immemorial – who is it? Suicide? Yes, indeed, it is Suicide.

Suicide has been steadfastly following me. She has always been with me. I have seen her with me since I reached the age of discernment (when did I reach the age of discernment?). However, I believe it is inaccurate to say that Suicide has been consistently following me. It would be more accurate on my part to say that she was born with me, as my inseparable shadow and timeless companion. I must acknowledge that though she was born with me, she is far more beautiful than I am. This isn't unusual, as everyone's suicide is far more alluring than they are. A thought or concept that is rare and is hence beautiful is undoubtedly superior to the small or the large intestine. What else is a human being other than their small or large intestine? If a human being is something other than these undesirable things, I am not aware of it.

I often find Suicide sitting before me, a smile flickering across her face. It is a compassionate smile.

Rarely does her smile betray any trace of a sneer; it happens only when my shamelessness and stupidity become intolerable even to myself. Suicide's smile, with its steep curves and sharp corners, always rests upon a cool, limpid lake. But the lake is not of natural origin. Suicide has painstakingly constructed it herself, breaking through huge, towering mountains, skilfully lifting the debris of massive rocks with her industrious, adept and sincere hands.

However, my treacherous shamelessness and deceit consist in the fact that I have always ignored Suicide. I have never given her the attention she deserves. Moreover, I have often strolled towards her beautiful lake with a certain disdain and indifference.

Though I encountered and endured many misfortunes and peculiar humiliations, I confronted them brazenly. It was like water off a duck's back. I transformed myself into a pitcher with a smooth façade, on which nothing could settle. The world is but such a place. It is absolutely hollow. Utterly void of all possibilities, the world contains nothing. I feel intensely that I did not come here of my own volition. I was poured into the world like water from a discoloured earthen jug. And now I am continuously growing turbid and murky here. Everything else, aside from growing turbid and murky, remains beyond my control. 'The impurity from the body flawlessly merged with the clay.' It seems to be a line from someone's poem. It may be a line from my own poem. None but I could conceive such an absurd and nonsensical thought.

The myriad fictitious tales that circulate about the world hold no modicum of truth. The teeming throng of people, their relationships, class conflicts, social injustices, armed conflicts, love and hatred, terrorism, political and economic disparities and so many other nonsensical things – they are all mere dreams seen by the human beings of another planet on this desolate plane of the Earth since time immemorial. They are the upturned pictures suspended in this world. They have been making dedicated efforts to improve this world for thousands of years, but their truth amounts to nothing more than a futile obsession. It's like throwing daggers at the pictures suspended in the air. I have come to know all this not just out of the blue. However, I am not a Sufi, Wali or Dervish. To be frank, I am a foul and malicious coward. For the cultivation of Jñāna, intuition and for gaining insight into the world, I never looked for a forest to wander in, a cave to retreat into, a leopard skin to sit on, or the Great Names of the Almighty to invoke.

The reality is that a cold sweat has afforded me this intuitive understanding. This cold sweat spouts from the unfathomable and incredible depth of my body, from the dark, subtle and fibrous recesses running through its pores.

The cold sweat spurts in a manner that makes me feel as if my very existence, with all its hidden potential, is bursting forth, tearing through my skin and breaking my bones. It is a form of destruction. It carries a peculiar odour, somewhat similar to the smell of blood. This cold sweat adheres to no specific time, season or day. It bursts forth without any warnings in every season, whether the freezing cold of winter, the rainy season or the oppressive humidity of summer. At times, while in a standing posture, I sense a scorching gust of wind brushing against my chest, arms and shoulders even in the midst of winter's icy grip. Then, deep beneath the sweater, the delusive approach of the cold sweat is heard. The sweat unexpectedly loses its way within the intricate labyrinth of winter. I slip my right hand beneath my sweater and reach it under my vest, attempting to catch hold of the melancholic bead of sweat right near my heart on the left side. Although my hand fails to grab it, yet its dull colour, like some unseen colour of a butterfly, leaves its traces on my finger.

I always have a sudden premonition of the impending arrival of this sweat, exactly as the worms and insects residing inside the Earth sense an imminent seismic wave. Even during the oppressively sultry weather, a mild dizziness swirls me like a forlorn whirlwind around the Earth in the dark gust of an unseen wind. My heart and pulse quicken in that moment, as if engaged in the grandest race against all the clocks suspended on the desolate walls of the world.

I am overwhelmed by a profound sense of restlessness and anxiety. At first, my heart feels a simmering heat while the left shoulder experiences a gloomy warmth. Then my feet begin to turn cold. I start treading on snow. Subsequently, my hands grow numb. A mysterious tremor grips my heart, hands and feet. I imagine myself to be made not of bones and flesh but of snow. An illusion, a mere assumption ...

Exactly at that moment, the inverted pictures hanging on the aerial walls of the world transform into shadows and lazily meander through the darkness of their dreams. I am gripped by the feeling that I am going to die. The sounds of me turning onto my other side and planting my foot on the earth echo, making me feel as if they are coming from miles away.

Incredibly, I gain an immediate intuition that the 'world', this damned world, is a hopelessly empty place. My eyes search in vain for tears to mourn the world's pitiable emptiness. But they fail to find tears. The eyes are incapable of holding within them tears as tall as a human being. Almost wide with wonder, my eyes fix their gaze into the space. Though vacant and open, they remain in a state of slumber.

Then she comes hopping on her tender toes to sit on my chest. The word 'she' refers here to my Suicide whom I have always attempted to ignore and forget. It is Suicide that wipes away the enigmatic sweat, tinged with the smell of blood, which spouts from my body. The rocks tumbling within the confines of the body come to a halt, and the earthquake ceases. The world once more gathers its myriad false faces fallen to the ground, and stands resolute in its concrete form. I breathe a sigh of relief, feeling relaxed with a strategy and a weapon at hand, even if I defer using the weapon to a later day.

But I know that the sweat will spurt out again, haunting my body like spectres. At any moment, I may be caught unawares by a perplexing yet dull heat in my temples, whether I am walking along the road or chewing a morsel of food. It leaves me blank, compelling me to lean against a tree or a wall with my head spinning and my feet wobbling. The clamorous uproar around me transforms into an unintelligible babel of voices drifting to my ears from a distant place. I must always be prepared to welcome this cold sweat. In such moments, Suicide stands beside me like a loyal and brave sentinel.

CHAPTER TWO

THE WIND THAT EVENING WAS VERY PLEASANT. SUCH breeze blows in my small town only after sunset – it touches both bodies and trees. During the daylight hours, however, it merely stirs clothes hung on the clotheslines.

Seated beside her, I gazed fixedly at the descent of her blue dupatta, slipping languidly from her bosom. A dark corner of the sky peeped inside through the window. Perhaps there was a patch of cloud over there. The food was laid out on the table. She was insistent on serving me the meal so meticulously prepared by her. In the crystal bowl before me shimmered the golden gravy, with a large white bone floating in it. As she extended the bowl to me, urging me 'to hold it and eat', I noticed that the colour of her hands bore a resemblance to the colour of the gravy. Her hands were yellowish up to the elbows, tinged with the faint hue of turmeric. Her forearms had a subtle sallowness. Her face is broad, its features tinged with masculinity. Her eyes were exceptionally large, so much so that they seemed to me as hollow as the world is wide.

I used my foot to savour the taste of her body – it was like the slightly bitter-sweet flavour of a chocolate. On rubbing my skin against hers like a fish brushing against another, I discovered the unique sensation and taste of her bosom. I have never done anything in a straightforward manner. Dogs and snakes lack taste buds, and whether I was more like a dog or a snake, I couldn't discern the taste of anything immediately. Immersed in the pool of vulgar desires, I found myself merely jumping, leaping or creeping within its confines.

As she urged me 'to hold the bowl and eat' while looking at me with her large and empty eyes, an unexpected sensation swept over me. I sensed its imminent arrival – my earlobes grew hot, and a tingling sensation coursed through my arms and legs. The wind blowing outside came to an abrupt halt. The corner of the sky peeping in through the window disappeared into the gloom, and the golden gravy shimmering in the crystal bowl was enveloped in darkness. It dawned on me that a spell of dizziness was about to overtake me. In a panic I clutched the chair's arms tightly and grounded my shoes firmly on the rough floor. Amidst the throes of life-threatening distress, I forced a smile and looked into her eyes. I don't know from where two white and sharp-pointed bones found their way to rest within her eyes.

She stood up and left, cradling the bones in her eyes with delicate care. I felt as if she were a small and narrow rivulet that meanders and vanishes abruptly into the mist and haze emanating from her own banks.

My entire body crawled with cold sweat. I buried my nose in my shirt and sniffed – the same old, unmistakable smell of blood lingered there. In that fleeting moment, the whole world once again became utterly barren, desolate and void.

CHAPTER THREE

I ALWAYS LEFT HER HOUSE LIKE A DOG, TAIL TUCKED between legs, and with a lingering thread of her dirty blue dupatta in my mouth. I never let the thread fall to the ground. If it accidently slipped from my mouth and touched the earth, dust or mud, I would immediately draw it back to my snout with each powerful breath I took. Each breath in, each breath out, in and then out. Love falls to the ground. Each time, it rises again. These lifeless veils can only be sustained throughout one's life by walking on all fours like a dog. Such is the nature of love – it has become enmeshed in the tangle of grass and straw of a mossy pond. Love has not faded away, but it has succumbed to the inner misgivings. Love always finds itself ensnared in misunderstanding. It remains unsure of which way it has to go. The lines of love perpetually spiral into a whirlpool. Hatred and lust are better for they never fall prey to misunderstanding and doubt. Their manoeuvres, principles and rules are transparent. They firmly recognise their boundaries, rights and obligations, expressing them briefly but candidly. It is love alone that remains trapped in doubt and suspicion, perpetually soaked in fear.

It is your ability to breathe, the function of your lungs, which not only justifies your continued existence on this hopelessly gloomy and absurd Earth but also confronts the world's shamelessness with an even greater shamelessness.

That evening, however, I came out of her house, zigzagging my way on two feet like a wretchedly lousy pig. I clearly saw the two white and pointed bones in her eyes and distinctly felt that my heart, beneath the left side of my perspiration-soaked chest, was the inevitable target of those bones. It seemed like a daunting task to protect my heart from those bones. Filled with dread and seeking some sort of protection against those bones, I affixed to my treacherous eyes two or three strands of pig hair which usually lie in my pocket reserved for such desperate occasions.

I staggered along the darkened streets, relying on walls for support. My legs were unsteady. I also felt as though my entire existence hung precariously from a nail driven into my back, swaying and fluttering in the air like a dirty blue shirt of grief, in its pocket the sweet biscuit stolen for love crumbled to pieces. Who was I to feed this biscuit to?

The bitterness of this relationship became apparent to me only later, much the same way a bitter taste is felt only when it hits the back of the tongue. The simple and benign sweetness of that biscuit could not dispel the bitterness of love.

As I swayed on my feet, soaked in perspiration, I found myself diving into the deep sea of intuition. Suicide, my inseparable shadow, whispered softly in my ear. On occasions of crucial importance, she whispers in my ear much like those select slaves of the King of Rome who, as part of their solemn duty at the coronation ceremony, softly intoned in the King's ear, 'This shall not last for ever.'

Suicide directed my attention to the sombre, smoke-laden whistle of a train traversing a distant landscape. 'Let us be run over by the train,' Suicide suggested. I agreed and began my journey towards the outskirts of the city where the railway tracks stretched out endlessly. I have always believed that there is no more fitting option for suicide than standing resolute on those very railway tracks. To me, considering alternatives such as drowning in a river or well, wielding a blade, hanging oneself or resorting to sleeping pills defies the essence and dignity of suicide. These methods seem simply imprudent. In fact, suicide derives a peculiar satisfaction in witnessing everything crumble to pieces, exactly like the Creator of the universe who derived pleasure in tearing the cosmos to pieces. People say, the Creator will dismantle this cosmos once more, shattering it into pieces and sending everything flying in the air.

Personally, I believe when a train packed with passengers hurtles towards its destination at a high speed and collides with your motionless body on the railway tracks, your body in that moment becomes one with the velocity of the passengers sleeping or seated in the compartments of the train, much like a stone thrown from outside into a moving train. Leaving the passengers far behind then and rendering their journey meaningless, your body reaches its destination in a fleeting instant, whereas no one knows when the poor passengers will arrive at theirs.

To sit down on the railway tracks is a carnival. It is a celebration of suicide. In contrast, other methods just leave your decaying body behind, destined to rot in solitary obscurity. I condemn and curse all other alternative modes of suicide.

Regretfully, I did not venture further down that fateful path. I could not see the dirt track that wound its way across the city, terminating at the railway tracks. Perhaps, this misstep was partly because of the profoundly dark night and partly because my vision was obscured by the two shameless strands of pig hair.

This behaviour of mine seemed strange to Suicide. But she did not utter a word. Instead, she simply slipped into my trousers' pocket, settling there like an innocent domestic squirrel. Since then, it has made a habit of sticking out its angelic face from my pocket, wistfully gazing at this empty world in a quiet and contemplative mood.

On my return, with the railway tracks now behind me, I noticed that the small piece of blue dupatta in my mouth felt feeble and flimsy. It seemed to dissolve like poison in my mouth.

Have my lips turned blue?

CHAPTER FOUR

IT IS A BIT OF AN ENIGMA, ONE THAT ELUDES THE GRASP of the thick human skull. My wife does not love me. Perhaps her dreams are attached to someone else. But she is happy in my company and harbours no desire to leave me and go anywhere else. On the other hand, the woman with pale yellow hands and vacant eyes loves me from the depths of her heart. However, she is not happy in my company. She yearns to sever ties with me, while I wish things to continue as they are. I desire no change in the current state of affairs, preferring to prolong my sins and cowardice. Such is the nature of things in this world; it's like putting marbles into a box and spinning them – who can predict which marble will collide with which one within the box? What becomes of a miniscule particle of dust caught in a whirlwind? Has anyone ever truly known this?

I believe I am responsible for both the fat around my wife's hips and the radiant glow on her face. Likewise, I am accountable for the yellowness of that woman's hands and the emptiness in her eyes. These are the evidence of my sins. I have been a sinner since time immemorial. The tale of my sins forms a tiny chapter within the saga of my childhood. A person who has suffered a severe head injury is susceptible to forgetting anything at any moment, whether it is humiliation, love or hatred. Both religion and this world are obscured by the nauseating churn of his heart and drowsy eyes. But he remembers his sins, even if he cloaks them in his mind as virtuous deeds. As I reflect on my sins, it feels as if my left shoulder is dislocated, causing a dampness to settle in my armpit.

Another irony is that all of my sins were like fruits with stones within. You can count the stones of these fruits after you have eaten them. The stones lie scattered before you – some on plates, others on newspapers, and some strewn on the floor. These sucked-out, ugly and repulsive stones soaked in your saliva continue to roll ludicrously across the floor. Why couldn't I have been allotted safe and abundant sins, like fleshy fruits without stones? The opposite happened to me: a list, an enumeration has always haunted me like a spectral presence. Everything can be counted: the deep furrows of a frown, a strand of hair knotted in anger, and the white, sharp-pointed bones lodged in the eyes and jutting out of them. The notion that lust is the sole driving force behind sins is entirely founded on a grave misconception. I have always viewed the bundle of my sins as the mark of my piety. In fact, those sins, misdeeds and thefts were my virtues. They brought me silent and great rewards. Every virtuous act has to be done discreetly. This was both the path and the law of true love. It was this understanding that led me to crossbreed the seeds of sins and love, planting a hybrid sapling that eventually grew into an acacia tree. Is it any less significant that an acacia tree also has a shadow exactly like mine? I have been contemplating changing my shadow's colour for quite some time now, giving my black shadow lying on the ground a coat of red or green paint; or should I consider squatting down to coat it with a paste of white chalk, creating unique shadows for each day and each moment. After all, a shadow is not merely a simple line drawing. A shadow does not originate from a tall, towering, short or stout figure; it originates from its inherent black hue. Since time immemorial, this black colour, flowing into light from the body of a poor human being, not only erodes his shape and features but also washes away his yearnings, sorrows, wounds and head injuries. It is, therefore, imperative for this shadow to keep changing colours, for in doing so, it can leave some clue about the human soul's sorrows and joys. What does it matter how crude, vibrant or gaudy the colours are? Human sorrows are no less crudely offensive and garish than these colours. Through specific hues of the shadow, mysteries can be unveiled as to how human sins became sanctified. But the recognition of sins and virtues through the blackness of the shadow seems to remain elusive. That is why I have, in a cowardly manner, kept my love separate, just as I have kept my sins apart. So, what wrong did I do? It is an extraordinary rock on which no moss will grow. It is a white mound of snow, an immense and pure glacier.

Deplorably, cartoons and caricatures are made even of love and virtues. This so-called sensible and wise world recognises every face only when it is portrayed as a cartoon. Love, when depicted as cartoon, takes on the shape and appearance of sins, perhaps appearing even more horrifying than a sin. Hence, it becomes essential for one to keep love apart. Every villainous flashlight must be wisely avoided.

However, even these efforts have proven futile now. All these attempts have been nothing more than a display of aiming and throwing knives at mere pictures. The crux of the problem was the body itself – the shadows emerge exclusively from the bodies, just as the sins. The cold sweat too comes from my own body, disrupting all my plans and endeavours. Resting in my trousers' pocket, Suicide becomes impatient and suddenly whispers in my ear, 'Let us consume poison.' As usual, I ignore its seductive whisper.

The body? Yes, the body – the body before its death. The true lesson of existence, it seems, can only be gleaned from observing a body before its death. What lesson can be learnt from seeing it in the grave? Who hasn't seen rats rotting away by the roadside? I am now compelled to think that the body is nothing but a fearsome, dark and mysterious abyss. Man resides within its confines. And so, he remains plagued by insecurity. Everything loses its way inside its deep maze. Even love will one day vanish into the obscurity of the body, like a hapless female rat falling terminally ill in her burrow, never to return. It is eventually reduced to a mere skeleton, or perhaps a handful of dust, fading into the vast expanse of the universe.

Through my sexual relationships with women, including my wife and the woman with pale hands, I have arrived at the profound realisation that the body is like a black hole. On nearing the black hole, not only love, but even sacrifices, empathy, various maladies and sufferings get sucked into it. No one and nothing can resist its magnetic pull. And the soul – the poor soul, whose idiom is meticulously written in the language of love and light constantly seeks its due attention, stuttering like an ignored tenant within the body. What else remains then?

What remains are the complaints and grievances, hopes that can't be fulfilled, newly forged hatred and the witches of those rivalries over which human beings have no control, for they emerge from the rotten skeleton of love. And what else …?

The illegitimate progeny of the bygone days; the ghosts of the past sitting within dust-laden, aged, discarded broken-down clocks, releasing soft peals of creepy laughter; an empty world cloaked in a massive, dust-coloured raincoat with numerous pockets; and countless suicides poking their faces out of those pockets while getting drenched in an unseen rain – these suicides are the inseparable shadows of human beings, the inseparable shadows of this world.

CHAPTER FIVE

I HAVE RETURNED TO MY WRETCHED, ACCURSED HOUSE. Suicide has crept out of my trousers' pocket to settle under my bed like a cat. As I lie beside my wife, I earnestly reflect on my follies. I feel as though some smoke is beginning to fill my eyes, perhaps tears are beginning to well up. Yes, indeed, they are tears. I dab at them with my index finger, and bring the tears to my tongue in order to taste them. They are vile and foul tears. Devoid of even salt, these tears are unabashedly shameless and obstinate. What good could possibly come from such tears? The past demanded a great sacrifice. To brood over the past was merely to engage in fresh foolishness. But everyone will repeat this folly time and again, for their first folly simply consisted in being born. Even my own first sin stemmed from my failure to reject my birth – undoubtedly, before that, I was relishing a blissful state in the realm of non-existence. An ignorance eliciting contempt, the lack of knowledge about the societal and cultural conditioning of countless languages and past lives misled my consciousness. Propelled by the desire to embrace existence, I entered my mother's womb. But what can I do now about the past? A man's past is synonymous with his destiny – the destiny on which lines are drawn. My destiny transformed into a small bag full of sand and was suspended from a dry banyan branch, enduring the blows and mighty punches of people. The bag full of sand was a punching bag to practice on. But only those who have been struck on their heads know the truth that from the sand-filled bag dripped blood in the dead of night. The blood dripping from it seeped into the roots of the banyan tree, and the Buddha's sorrows exacted sacrificial offerings for that blood. In sum, the fate, covered with blood, transformed into a liver which was excised from the body – the body never cared about this unfortunate fate.

Tired and fretful, I turned on my side, longing to cuddle up to my wife's fair and rosy body. But she stiffened in her sleep. She had no inkling that tonight once again I had returned home after hanging about a place dangerously close to the railway tracks. Still, shamelessly, I reached out to feel for my wife's deformed breast. One breast is noticeably different in size and shape from the other. My feelings seemed to have no effect on her, except that she turned on her side, her back now facing me. My wife is incapable of understanding anything. It is no use expecting anything from individuals who see with one ear or hear with one ear. In such people I have always perceived a natural defect. One ear of such characters differs from the other, just as one eye does from the other. Perhaps, one of every woman's two breasts is inherently different from the other.

As for me, ages have passed since both my eyes wept in unison. Both my ears join in the mournful sounds for centuries, and an equal weight of mucus flows from each nostril. Hence, it is only I who can witness this spectacle. The shimmering heat of the noontime sun, the swirling dust storms, the whirlwind of thirst, the white bones jutting into vacant eyes, the dizzy spells, the cold sweat and suicide – each makes its presence felt solely through my body. But the ear that is not the twin of the other ear, the eye which is not the companion of the other eye and the breast that is not the confidante of the other breast fail to capture this spectacle in its entirety. They cannot even watch the inverted pictures suspended in the void world. I feel an urge to hug my wife, but she is dreaming away on a separate multi-coloured pillow. Sleep eludes me. My wife wears lipstick even when asleep. Her lips are very thick. After applying red lipstick, she always keeps them slightly open, which makes her red lips look like two separate slices of an ugly watermelon, allowing the wind to sit between them. I will have to swallow the lovely blue pill that is kept on the head of the bed and is gazing fondly at me. 'My lovely pill!' I tenderly caressed the pill amid soft murmur, which wakes my wife. 'Why are you yelling? It is past midnight, can't you stay still?'

she says angrily. 'Oh, you woke up.' I say with an effort to press her shapely plump head against my stomach. But her entire body stiffens to an astonishing degree. And the air between my hungry, empty stomach and her plump head suddenly transforms into a hard, black rock. Suicide scampers like a mouse, rattling things under the bed. Then she falls motionless. Overcome by despondency, I pop the blue pill into my mouth. The pill, much like a compassionate, sweet stream of milk, satiates my jaded palate, soothing my throat.

I have come to understand that there are but two types of strengths in human beings. One manifests when a woman, enraptured by the passion of love, transforms the vigour of every bone in her body into an intoxication and becomes as light and delicate as air and dissolves into your embrace, resting her soft head on your shoulder with the tender softness of cotton. And the other takes form when the same woman stiffens her body and fiercely pushes your hands and head away, turning into a terrifying gust of scorching wind. Clumps of grizzled hair whirl around her arms. The bones floating in the gravy within the crystal bowl leap and settle in her gaze. A chilling black line looms up, drawn between you and her, leaving you to stare at her helplessly as she stands on the other side of that line. This is a dreadful power, hell-bent on devastating everything. When your woman wields this power to its utmost, the darkness from within your heart comes out and bounces to the walls. Then you are left like a tree swaying silently and melancholically in your own wind during an incredibly black night. This is a nasty wind. In your attempt to save yourself against this wind, you end up being more humiliated.

I have turned off the sleep-inducing bulb. Now it is utterly dark. It has become apparent to me in the darkness that I am starving. However, it's not from the burning sensation in my stomach that I have received this message. Darkness has been my teacher since time immemorial. A great mentor, it has shown me all these things – a pimple grown on the heart and a scratch inflicted by an unseen nail. It's darkness that revealed to me that the place in someone's heart once occupied by me had long since been filled. I also know that the source of the chilling perspiration of intuition is darkness itself. Now, the sleep has started overpowering me. However, it is with my drowsy eyes that I am playing chess in the darkness. I am playing a game of cards with my soul. How bright this world is! Everything, ranging from the depths of the nether world to the five senses of the ants crawling on the earth, is clearly within my sight now. The darkness is in possession of such a brilliant light that it has given rise to monotony and inertia. In this heavy and hard light of darkness, I have received a severe blow on my head. I can clearly see blood oozing out and congealing in clots, and can also see Suicide, whom I ignored, deferring my intention of dying, sitting pasted to my body.

I can observe the sacks of my sins – they are spotlessly white from within. But someone is dragging this sack across the rough floor, leaving behind a trail of blood trickling out of it. The floor grows dirty and wet. There is a pus-filled pimple growing inside an artery of my heart. Who is the one dragging the sack of my sins leaving in its wake a stream of raw blood across the floor? What a strange and despondent sound this movement emits! The darkness has deepened further, conveying a new message to me, that I am both anguished and emaciated. I wish to stay happy. I have craved for ages to remain extremely happy. This was why I had planted the seed of body in my barren and bleak soul living in the realm of non-existence. But has any soul ever been able to withstand the hellish weariness of happiness?

The joy that arose from loving and being loved, and the pleasure that was to be derived by treading the path of salvation, didn't quite manifest. In reality, precisely these paths of love and salvation often lead us to trouble. Love that doesn't allow the gratification of physical desires throws the soul into despondency – all the paths, including the path to salvation and redemption, terminate in a labyrinth. They don't actually head towards the direction where the arrow-shaped symbol is visible. The geography of the soul, its map, is impossible to contain in my tattered pocket. Though its history remains vivid because my memory is embedded like traffic lights at various intersections in the dreadful labyrinth of time.

This memory sometimes turns green and sometimes red. I respect these signals of my memory, and follow the directions they show. For ages, I have stood still before a red light at a crossroads. And then, I have found myself lying prostrate in the murky open drains in the winding alleys of my soul.

Amidst darkness, as I lay with my face down on the bed, I perceive a dreadful and cruel blow hurtling towards me. The dry soil of a strange planet begins to erode in the distant space, its lumps falling and striking my heart. The haze of its yellow dust mingled with blood has jammed my heart.

CHAPTER SIX

I STAY AWAKE IN THE DARKNESS THROUGHOUT THE night. As a result, I feel extremely drowsy in the morning. Like a raging flood, my wife jolts me awake. I sit up and nearly sleepwalk against the tide of sleep. With rheumy eyes, I write down the tale of my weary soul and paralysed hands and feet, contrasting it against the narrative of slumber. I convert the toilet's grey floor, the toothbrush, the razor and the foamy soap lather into metaphors symbolising readiness for the future. Disrupting the romantic tale spun around the slumber, sleep falls from my eyes like rheum. Light filters into my eyes aided by boiling hot tea, two biscuits, a tablet for blood pressure and the pink pill for depression.

But at night, sleep exacts its revenge upon me, retaliating for the morning's humiliation. Lurking in a distant corner, it waves its fist at me. It never goes too far away from me. It plays cat and mouse, slapping, teasing and nipping at me before darting away. I hear its poisonous laughter reverberating around the house.

It is my chest that bears the brunt of its malevolent and vile game, feeling as if weighed down by a huge stone. My eyes long to burn and my legs feel heavy. Just as the dawn is about to break, sleep finally infiltrates my eyes. But how can I say with absolute certainty that it is the same sleep that sucked my blood like a sorceress all through the night, or whether it is another sleep, its identical counterpart which drove away the sorceress and pitched a tent over my legs. It is also possible that this morning sleep has been created by my body itself. Much like how a silkworm spins silk, my drained-out body and head that have received a severe blow spin sleep. My entire life is filled with countless such mistakes, ironies and idiocies. What greater mistake could I have made than to possibly attack the sleep that is sympathetic towards me in the morning? All that has transpired in my life has been nonsensical and absurd. For instance, I always found myself immersed in a movie where each scene was disjointed from its accompanying dialogue – the dialogue came somewhat before or after the scene. The sound failed to synchronise with the scene. The sound drifted independently within the movie's frame, imparting language to every scene. Similarly, I encountered foreign movies in which the subtitles were either much delayed or ahead of the audio. This may have happened due to technical defects. But I have been encountering these things throughout my life. With my futile attempts, I have been rashly and awkwardly endeavouring to synchronise scenes and dialogues in films of an unfamiliar language. As a consequence, I have been undone and everything around me has descended into a disturbing and chaotic array. Scenes of hatred appeared first in the sequence of events, but I chose to overlay them with dialogues of love. Moreover, when love finally appeared in the sequence of events after a considerable time, I found myself listening to it or reading it in the voice of lust and desire. Everything – sorrow, joy, anger, vengeance, love, hatred, intoxication, sickness, sweat and madness – followed in a haphazard succession. The entire theatre was transformed into the theatre of the absurd. I feel miserable and frustrated, wondering why things never seem to happen to me as they do to other people. As a common man walks down the road, he catches sight of a white object flickering and approaching from a distance. He perceives it but he does not recognise it. However, as his senses converge, aligning and coordinating with each other, he comes to understand that the object in slow motion is in fact a white cow. But I could never successfully complete this natural journey from perception to realisation. To me, each step taken in this journey feels like nothing more than the rumbling of thunder and flashes of lightning in the sky. It is raining in the remote mountains, clouds are thundering and lightning is flashing. The scene of lightning flashes before my eyes, followed by the roar of thundering clouds. The actual damage has already been sustained, much before the sound is heard. But in my case, has destiny written a scene to accompany each and every sound?

After all, I had also heard the savage, ruthless sound of the blow in the generous darkness before I unexpectedly found my head bespattered with blood and mud.

As I squat on the floor, my eyelids droop, heavy with sleep. The dawn will surely be on the brink of breaking. The moon is no longer visible through the rear ventilator. Defeated by this shameless and vile world, it has descended into the slopes of the sky. So, the moon of this night also proved futile. It failed to realise its dangerous intentions, unable to destroy even my small city, let alone the world. All the chameleons are being dumped there, leaving the source of the dry well buried beneath the garbage, dead and lifeless debris. What should I do now? Shall I stay awake or go back to sleep?

The dawn is breaking, and a faint light is filtering through the ventilator. I will have to get up. In just a few minutes, my father's muttering and throat-clearing will jar my ears.

Defying sleep, now I must rise to my numb feet.

CHAPTER SEVEN

MY FATHER AND I HATE EACH OTHER. HE GLARES AT ME with loathing, and so do I. It is a silent contest of animosity. I will turn into him. My father is my future, and moving towards the future feels like landing a punch on the obscene mouth of time, knocking out all its teeth. Moreover, I am addicted to the bad habit of delivering punches. This habit is hard to break now.

In appearance, I have closely taken after my father. Tall and well-built, I resemble my father with my chocolaty complexion. Even my eyelids blink like his. However, the colour of his eyes differs from mine. His eyes are very small and brown, while mine resemble my mother's eyes. Her eyes are black and perhaps even larger than a cow's. One can even say that her eyes are grotesquely wide, bordering on the absurd. Other than this, I can be declared identical to my father from every angle. But the left side of my head bears a depression, a hollow emptiness like a pit. My father's head is perfectly circular, beautiful and unblemished.

Initially, I wasn't aware that my father also harboured hatred for me. It was only through the comprehensive study of my own hatred that I came to understand his reciprocal loathing. Hatred is a complex and esoteric branch of learning. Its principles and codes are as intricate as the codes of sorcery and necromancy. But once its rules are mastered, hatred transforms into a kind of mathematics whose formulae easily deflate not only the grand theories of Psychology, Anthropology and Sociology but also let the air out of the globe called 'world'.

As for my malignant hatred towards my father, it had perhaps taken root long before my birth, when I was just a foetus in my mother's womb. I must have been only about five years old when my father harshly punched my hand, causing all the peanuts in my fist to scatter to the ground. Peanuts irritate him. He feels irritated by anything that has shells or peels, as one must deal with the remnants after consuming the contents, and is inevitably left with the task of cleaning them up. Anyhow, when I was five, he flew into a rage and began to beat me severely. Desperate to shield me, my mother leapt to intervene but even she was pushed aside. Tears welled up in my mother's large eyes. After bashing me up, my father stormed out of the house. I did not weep at that time. However, amidst the blows rained on me by my father's hands, I felt as if I was running a fever – a fever that lies dormant in the bones like old, long-forgotten events. But then one day, it resurfaces on the skin determined to scorch the entire body.

No. I didn't weep at all. But yes, a wind persisted all through the night – it seemed as if the wind's throat was choked. Such winds often sweep through those drains that flow silently beneath the small, broken bridges over roads. I got stomach cramps. As I turned the tap on in the toilet, the air trapped in the mossy pipes rushed out, crudely mimicking a mournful wail. Water streamed out then, howling. It felt as though someone was imitating the sound of crying all around. Or perhaps someone was genuinely crying, but it lacked the usual cadence of weeping and the rhythm was broken. It seemed like someone's unsuccessful attempt at crying – a cry punctuated by stammers, a sound unable to cry, an unfinished construction. Perhaps it was the cry of a tapeworm which, buried under faeces, is finally flushed down the toilet with the rushing water in a filthy and dark drain.

It was in that haunting moment that the revelation of unfathomable hatred for my father dawned on me as I squatted down in that dark toilet. Since then, we have both been inextricably bound by a burning chain of animosity, forever fated to stay together.

CHAPTER EIGHT

MY MOTHER, FATHER AND I ARE ALWAYS ENTANGLED IN quarrels. Violent clashes often erupt between them. My mother's mother came from a lineage of meerasis. As my mother had received some education, she chose not to pursue her mother's profession of singing and dancing. My father, on the other hand, was a respectable man, coming of a noble feudal stock. I don't know how and where he exchanged amorous glances with my mother. Despite stiff opposition from his family, my father married her, and they established their own household on a separate street. But they soon discovered that their love for each other had vanished without a trace. Instead of the bonds of love, it was merely a line that joined them. They were entirely different from each other. However, without that connection, they had no individual identity.

My mother's face is slender but her forehead is round. Her nose is slightly thick and pug-like, and her eyebrows are almost non-existent. She seethes with immense pent-up anger. The way honey-bees express themselves by buzzing, in order to attract attention to the honey stored in their hives, my mother expresses her anger by beating the drum in a mournful rhythm. She had brought the drum from her mother's house solely out of her fondness for it. My father not only detested the idea of her playing the drum but also hated the very presence of it in our house. However, I have always sensed that my father is somewhat under my mother's heel. In their altercations and physical confrontations, my mother typically held the upper hand. But in my case, she would always become weak and submissive. Whenever he thrashed me, abused or clawed at my skin, she would falter in fiercely fighting him and defending me. The colour would drain from her face. This is a mysterious thing, but not so mysterious a thing. Between spouses, even more incomprehensible and bewildering phenomena often arise. It is the most unique relationship in this world, where to prove their mutual intimacy husband and wife have to sleep together in a state of undress. Despite this, both remain unable to fully trust each other. The husband does not know whether or not the foetus growing in his wife's womb is his own child, while the wife, even with the persistent nagging and pestering, cannot decide whether or not the flimsy strand of hair on her husband's neck belongs to her. This relationship is largely founded on sexual acts. Both partners immerse their respective identities in deep secrets in an effort to extend their individualities, which later proves to be a dried-up well. That's why desire fuelled by libido is always better than the sexual act, just as darkness is invariably better than light. In lust, human beings use each other as medicine to alleviate their pain, serving as bandages for each other's pus-filled wounds.

It is unfortunate that one day, even lust disappointingly evaporates from this relationship.

My mother's eyes, grotesquely large and black, not only appeared oddly disproportionate on her face, but also seemed disconnected from her raging anger, which made me think of the dreadful beehives. Her anger altered the colour of all her features.

My father clenched my mother's hair in anger and spat out, 'You are a bitch, a damned bitch.' My mother, firmly gripping the collar of my father's shirt with one hand, was hitting him with the other while calling him names, 'You are a pimp, a damn procurer.' My father kicked her and hurled obscenities at her. In anger, my mother kicked the ground disgustedly, sending the dust flying. She let go of the collar of my father's shirt, hit the ground and began to gasp for breath on the ground. Her hair, released from my father's grip, began to dance wildly on her copper-coloured face.

'You are a dog, a damned seed of a dog. You threw her down from the rooftop, didn't you? Her seven-month-old foetus miscarried. You are a sinner, you wretched impotent,' my mother yelled at the top of her voice. It seemed like she was about to go into convulsions.

Foaming at her mouth, she began tearing her clothes until she was nearly naked. Then she ran towards the door. Her naked hips wiggled in a dreadful way. My father followed her, quickly closing the door and barring my mother's way. He stood in front of her. 'Calm down, be quiet, speak quietly,' he urged amidst feelings of fright. He was out of his wits. My mother stared at him with her large, black eyes. Those eyes held no hint of anger, or perhaps they had, as always, a black rage in them. A stream of abuse continued to pour forth from my mother's mouth.

Recoiled in horror, I lay down on the bare floor, pulling a sheet over me. The cacophony of abuse gradually turned into filthy whispers. Gripped by fear, I remained there with my eyes shut tight. A drowsy sensation began to envelop me. I saw the black wall again. There was a rift in the wall with scrubs growing out of it. From this rift a dirty and murky light was streaming in, the kind of illumination that is produced by burning garbage by the roadside. Perhaps, or rather undoubtedly, this light resides within my closed and weeping eyes.

It is pouring with rain. In the dark and desolate rainy night, the roof of a dilapidated house leaks badly. Dressed in a white shalwar and perhaps a black kurti, there stands a minor girl on the decrepit roof tiles of a stilted house, struggling to mend the leakage. The slope of the tiled roof is treacherous, and the tiles are covered with moss. Lightning flashes across the sky in distant valleys. And the rainwater is streaming through the roof tiles, much like it flows through drainpipes. A dog is getting drenched in this rainwater, shivering intermittently. The shadow of the drenched dog falls on the wall in front of the house. Suddenly, a tall shadow appears right beside the girl leaning to mend the leakage in the roof tiles. This is my father. He seizes the girl, pulling her towards him with force. In the distance, a cat starts whimpering on a parapet in the rain. He whispers something in her ear. The girl shakes her head in denial. He says something again, and the cat whimpers once more. The girl screams loudly, saying, 'No! I won't go to anyone else's house. I will raise it myself.' My father tightens his grip over her hand. The girl's white shalwar flutters in the wind. She wrenches her hand out of his grip and steps ahead towards the slope. My father follows her, walking carefully on the mossy roof tiles. The girl advances, her feet unsteady on two wobbly tiles. As she begins to slip, she throws her hands in the air in a desperate attempt to regain balance and secure her footing. She resembles a scarecrow standing in a desolate field. But propelled by a powerful, rain-soaked gust of wind, she slips from the mossy slope with her hands outstretched. She falls down on the dog getting wet in the rainwater. The sound of the rain gets drowned out by her piteous, hysterical screams. The dog barks with all its might. The rain becomes heavier.

My father's long shadow on the tiled rooftop has disappeared. The girl twists and writhes in the muddy courtyard, as the rain pours down turning the mud into slush. The girl's white shalwar is splashed with blood and torn flesh, which the dog soaked in rainwater now sniffs and licks. The rain has become even heavier, duller and discoloured. The dog now jumps and swoops on the girl's shalwar like a predatory wild cat. In this dull and discoloured rain, at the last turn of the alley, a well's parapet comes into view. The shroud of the rain on the hazy parapet has gradually obscured all – the hazy parapet, the dog, the girl, the blood and the agonising screams. Only the last turn of the alley, after which the street terminates in a dead end, remains clearly visible. At the end of this dead-end street stands the well, where a cat wails mournfully on the desolate parapet.

I am no longer crying. I wake up to the sound of a drum. My mother, seated beside me on the bare floor, is beating her drum. Amidst mournful beats, she softly lets out abuse. These swear words are the refrains that she rhythmically plays on the drum. Each musical instrument has its own unique, private song. This is the black drum's song, which has been composed by abusing and hurling curses at the destiny of human beings. Unable to endure the relentless drum and its refrains, blue lines get etched on human destiny. My mother is cursing and abusing as if she were letting out whisperings. As she whispers, she sometimes also laughs at the beat of the drum with the entire blackness of her lungs. It is a broken, cracked laugh, a dry laugh, resembling the sound of heavy footsteps crushing brittle, dry and dead twigs.

CHAPTER NINE

MY FATHER EVENTUALLY WAKES UP FROM SLEEP. HE kicks the drum as hard as he can. The drum has come out of my mother's grip. It tumbles down to the ground, producing a series of thumping sounds as it rolls away. Its challenge continues unabated. As the drum rolls down to a corner and comes to a standstill against the wall, it exudes a warm glow of satisfaction and a radiant sense of accomplishment, as if it has completed its great song and surrendered it to silence. And it too has fallen quiet. My father has again grabbed my mother by her hair. And he is tugging at it continuously. 'You whore, haramzadi, you slept with that fugitive soldier, the one who died a wretched dog's death, shot by the bullets of military police. So, to wear his dirty uniform, you stripped off all your clothes in front of him.' My father bangs my mother's head on the floor, adding, 'A wretched bitch, your lust knows no bounds. The bastard child of a meerasi, you were counting my sins. Look at your own sin. Look at this bastard. I will rub your head into the ground. I will choke this bastard to death too.' He then lets go of my mother's hair. Panicked, my mother squats down on the floor. She is no longer hurling obscenities. She is perhaps crying softly while saying, 'No! This is wrong. He is your child.' My mother is trembling. 'You liar, cheat, whore, this is the seed of the same dog, of the same fugitive soldier,' says my father and kicks my mother's back. She quakes as if she is merely a shadow. 'Believe me. For God's sake, it's your own child, your own blood, your heir,' pleads my mother. Her words are clearly audible amidst sobs and whispers, but the lips of the shadow do not move visibly.

Frightened out of my wits, I hide my face in the sheet again. I am scared. I want to sleep again. I feel sleepy. Light is again entering my eyes and has illuminated the same black wall and the same crack overgrown with wild plants. A dirty flame of fire emanates from the crack, the flame that is produced by burning garbage by the roadside.

In this dirty strip of light, a small city becomes visible. The city, its winding streets, high and low, and small and large buildings are all wrapped in the bitter cold and silent cloak of fog. No light is visible in any building. But this darkness is not just due to the black cold, the panes of the windows and the ventilators of every house are covered with black paper so that the planes of the hostile country cannot find any trace of the human settlements. No sound is heard anywhere. No one comes out. This is a blackout. The war continues. Warplanes repeatedly fly past the rooftops of the houses with their terrifying roars. An order has been issued to turn off the lights of all houses just after the evening falls. Sometimes, the army patrols the streets stomping on the ground with their heavy boots, and if there is even a slight hint of light in someone's house, they knock on the door and warn against keeping any kind of light on, proceeding with caution and vigilance. They cannot tolerate even a glimmer of light on the hearth.

After the passage of several watches of the night in the dark and terrifying silence, a hushed and panicky knock is heard on the dark doors of a house. My father gets up noiselessly, and like a cat, he tiptoes to the door quietly, opening it carefully and cautiously. The door does not creak on its hinges. But a shadow enters through the door. The shadow is bruised and tattered from place to place. Whispering softly into my mother's ear, my father says, 'He is from among our brethren. He belongs to our faith. We will give him refuge.' The shadow crouches into a corner and sits down. My mother's eyes gleam in the darkness like those of a cat. They are gleaming on the walls and their corners like a flickering torch or like two shining marbles. The gleam of those eyes turns the shadow first into a negative of a photo and then gradually into a beautiful illuminated image. Time has moved a bit forward in the frame of the film. The age in the bodies has increased a bit more. The freezing cold has abated, the terror has subsided and the darkness has thinned. What in the world is there that brings no benefit? Even the war has its benefits. The dreadful carnage and genocide in the war have annihilated large swathes of human population. The Earth is transforming into a forest. The environmentalists are satisfied thinking what better way there could be to maintain the temperature of the universe and the ecological balance. The blazing flames of war have illuminated the dark city plunged in blackout. War has also made my mother's eyes glint. A new gleam sparkles in her black eyes. Her lips are now like blooming lotus. She has begun to wear green bangles that look like fresh green grass against the colour of her soil-like skin. In her flimsy brown hair, repeatedly tugged and pulled by my father's hands, she has learnt to wreathe white flowers. She has started singing soft and sweet songs on her drum – they mimic the frightening roars of the warplanes zooming across the sky. How much time has passed? It has been ages since the bullets were fired on the distant border. Once again, in the pitch dark night, in the blackout, there is a knock on the same door. It is not just one knock, it is many knocks. These are not knocks. These are the weighty kicks of the heavy boots and sharp bayonets that are breaking the frail wood of the door down. The beautiful, illuminated picture transforms into negative, and then suddenly into a bruised and tattered shadow. Under the cloak of the black cold, the shadow creeps out from the rear ventilator of the house. A little later, at the last turn of the dark alley, near the well, several bullets are fired one after another. The jarring thumps of the heavy boots cause the street to crack, and several holes are burned through the dirty, torn uniform. My mother's eyes become desolate and colourless. There are no tears in them. Tears have come to settle in her eyes, like a quiet wind. My mother's lips resemble burnt crops.

My eyes are opened by my father's dreadful snores. I have pulled my face out from the sheet. My mother is sitting on the floor, with her head tucked between her legs, and silent. Who knows how much of the night has passed? I have peacefully hidden my face in the sheet again. Sleep is going to overtake me now. I know they will not fight any more tonight. In deep sleep, I have felt my mother lovingly kiss my forehead. She is smiling, and in her black eyes, there is a shining tear as tall as I am. In that tear, a melancholic pomegranate tree sways. In the balmy breeze of that forlorn, melancholic tree, my sleep has grown even deeper. I am sleeping like an infant. I am munching on handfuls of peanuts. I am truly sleeping.

CHAPTER TEN

WHEN I WOKE UP THE SUN HAD ALREADY CLIMBED high. My mother was not on the floor. She was not in the house either. She had gone somewhere. Her drum lay silent in one corner. My father had been dashing around with other people from the neighbourhood, searching for her. She couldn't be found. I rushed out of the house. It was the autumn season. Dry leaves and twigs were being trampled under my feet. And from them came the sound of my mother's dry laughter. I ran and ran and perhaps reached the city's border where there is a desolate mound of soil. I saw my mother on the mound in the distance. But she disappeared, then resurfaced, and vanished again. My mother then shrank to a dot, moving further and further away until she disappeared completely behind the mound where the graves of war prisoners lay. After that, she never hove into my sight. It was after then that I began to keep a knife hidden in my knickers. I wave the knife, drawing lines in the space. I want to kill my father, and smear his blood on my face.

What is all this? Is it a comedy or tragedy? Perhaps both? But who is the protagonist of this drama? Certainly not me. Even though I have written the script of this drama, I am unable to appear on this stage even as a villain. I am but a gloomy and dismal shadow. Quaking in the limelight on the stage is neither the shadow of a human nor any object. This is not a shadow meant to be visible in light. It is the shadow of a filthy abuse suspended in the air. It is the shadow of a shamefaced wind sitting in the darkness with its head burrowed into its arms and shins. Therefore, the scream of tragedy can never be heard on stage. The feeble, discomfited scream, tumbling amidst kicks, never aligns with the songs written for a tragedy. It has no rhythm, no melody and no harmony. It is only the muffled, unrecognisable voice of a stomach worm. It is the scream that turns this tragedy into a comedy. So the grand, moral stage of the tragedy kicks it away with contempt, ordering its departure. The curtain falls, then rises again. But the shadow remains seated, bowing in darkness. The theatre continues. The despairing scream is unable to even garner a single applause. The scream whimpers, bursts into laughter and then goes mad. It begins to crawl towards the mad, dirty wind from which it was born. There in the darkness it remains slumped, and here the theatre goes on.

CHAPTER ELEVEN

AFTER MY MOTHER'S DISAPPEARANCE, MY FATHER began to raise me in the house filled with hatred. He cooked my food, washed my clothes and taught me how to pronounce words correctly. He made me solve maths problems, especially those involving the compound interest. But every time he did something for me, he glared at me balefully, his eyes ablaze with seething hatred. He incessantly addressed me as the 'bastard' who was only growing fatter by indulging in food while becoming increasingly dull in the matters of learning and studies. I started to keep my knife close at hand. Every day I pondered how I could kill him with that knife. Just with that knife.

One day, he tied me to the electric pole in the street and brutally beat me in front of everyone. My crime: I had made a lewd gesture towards a girl slightly older than me in my neighbourhood. The truth is that it had been going on for some time. I would stand on the rooftop of my house, and she would also come up to her roof on seeing the opportune moment. Although our houses were a little far apart, our rooftops conveniently faced each other directly, and even from a distance, we could see each other clearly. She would often watch my lewd gestures with great interest, and would double up with laughter. One day, the people of the neighbourhood saw our game. The girl was declared innocent, and the blame fell squarely on me. To maintain his prestige and reputation in the neighbourhood, my father decided to punish me publicly.

In the old days, my grandfather used to have tillers of his land bound to the trunk of the trees and mercilessly thrashed. This upbringing was ingrained in my father's blood. The black, hard iron pillar had live electricity wires suspended above it. A persistent hum came from the white porcelain insulators perched atop the pillar. On that summer night, a high watt bulb shone intensely, its powerful light burning within a large white ceramic protective case. Moths swarmed around, dancing madly in the glaring brightness. Due to the light, insects and moths, countless lizards had appeared on the wall behind the pole. He hit me only with his feet. Sometimes, an electric shock from the pillar, its charge flowing from the ground through the lightning rod, would convulse my body, sending jolts down the spine. I did not remember the taste of my mother's milk, but the tremors inside her womb came back vividly to my mind. Certainly, at that moment, I should have cried in my mother's voice, but

I didn't cry at all. Instead, I imagined myself as a black iron pillar, which was displaying a unique demonstration of strength by holding up its back against another iron pillar. Tiny insects were entering my ears, mouth and nose, and lizards clinging to the wall behind me seemed to chuckle at the spectacle. Hatred can be confronted only with hatred, not with tears. Instead of lingering in the eyes, it is better for the tears to enter the intestines and stay hidden there.

The years rolled by. My father's age began to decline. His habit of swearing at me gradually decreased. His voice grew feebler day by day, and he began to get bouts of cough. I started to grow into a tall, sturdy and strapping young man. But I continuously failed in school exams. I had sexual relationships with several girls in my neighbourhood. To them, I resembled a film hero from an old movie, except that my head was slightly depressed on the left.

During that tender age, I had some interest in religion. But as I grew older, my heart gradually grew cold towards it. I stopped going to places of worship even on special occasions. Because even now, going there I feel as if I am bound to the same black iron pillar, and a black whip is slowly creeping towards me. I began to feel scared of going there.

Sometimes, in a state of great anxiety, I feel as if I once had an island that is now submerged in water. On that submerged island, not even a trace of my footsteps will be left now. All the soil will have been eroded, and in place of those footprints, a shoal of fish with drowsy eyes will be rubbing their gills. I often stand in front of the mirror, calling out to my memory, my faithful dog. But it is wandering somewhere else. My sunken island does not resurface. I am waiting for a lunar eclipse that will stir up such a tide which will cause my island to re-emerge from the depths and settle in my mirror. With froth in my mouth and teeth clenched, I am perpetually collecting my old shadows. I sweep the mirror so that I can gather the remnants of the past shadows.

But soon I realise my foolishness and mistakes. There are no shadows in the mirror. The mirror holds only your reflection, a possessed monkey imitating your actions. You raise a blow, and it is aimed at your own face. This is an image, a boring and mean drama full of malice and hatred. It always confronts you like an inveterate and eternal enemy, devoid of all possibilities except for hostility. It is what you are. But as for the shadow – it is your solitary companion. It never appears before you to laugh. When you raise a blow, your shadow seeks to extend that blow into the infinity. Its dark or blurred lines are enriched with endless possibilities. They always meander on the edges of your body, guarding the body and widening it as well. Separating itself from the body, the shadow not only stands before you but sometimes it lurks around you, sometimes behind you, sometimes to the left or right, and sometimes within you. And sometimes the shadow surrenders itself faithfully to you, completely synchronising its flowing lines with the geometry and contours of your body.

Still, a shadow has its own world, a separate existence. It owes nothing to the mirror or light for its existence. It mocks the light. Through its black lines, changing lights, shifting angles and the ascending and descending sun, it constantly alters its contours, yearning to go elsewhere. It wraps up all its darkness on a grand stage of tragedy, ready to play its magnificent role, like an actor who not only embodies his character but also transcends the boundaries of his performance, breaking and flowing outwards. And I …? What else do I do these days? I sweep with a broom in hand, gathering shadows. I sweep them to fill my empty basket. But my submerged island does not resurface, I foam at the mouth, my teeth clench against each other and I start getting fits.

My father started putting around my neck amulets, talismans and threads tied into knots after blowing incantations over them. They were so heavy that I started to walk with a stoop, struggling to catch my breath. He rushed me to all sorts of physicians and hakims. My house was heaped with colourful pills. After taking these pills, I started to sleep peacefully. But they brought no significant improvement to my condition. Instead, I began to gain weight, and my misdeeds multiplied and lust intensified. I completely neglected my studies. My father no longer prevented me from doing anything. Perhaps he had resolved his past dilemma of whether I was his own seed or an illegitimate offspring. It seemed he had reluctantly accepted me as his unfortunate progeny. I resembled him exactly in appearance, but deep down, my sixth sense told me that he still harboured hatred for me. This hatred festered like an abscess, spreading its pus throughout the recesses of his being. I saw him many times dusting my mother's drum and secretly weeping, but it did not diminish my hatred for him. On the contrary, it only intensified the animosity. I increased the frequency of brandishing my knife, drawing lines in the air to the extent of madness. I started throwing a dagger at the inverted picture of my father.

CHAPTER TWELVE

SOME QUACK FOOLISHLY SUGGESTED TO MY FATHER that he should marry me off, it will rein in my madness. My father, utterly fed up with me by then, arranged for me to get married, but only after considerable effort, relying on much fabrication. On the night of my wedding, my father roughly pushed me, with hatred and malevolence, into the room the bride was waiting in. She was a short, plump, fair-skinned girl. Sitting on the bridal bed, she resembled a large, inflated red balloon, lovely enough to attract children to play with it. I fell asleep after a perfunctory act of love-making. I had already swallowed several blue pills, so I succumbed to a deep sleep. Alas! My special dreams eluded me that night. The reason was the presence of another head sharing my pillow, the strange puffs of her breath and the repulsive smell of saliva drooling from the mouth. Genuine dreams desire a solitary body. They also require loneliness. They descend from unseen voids for the lonely, sleeping person. However, they retreat when they find some other head sharing the pillow. In their hasty departure, they leave behind twisted trails and curves similar to the lines left by swiftly drifting objects on the surface of water. These trails and curves offer no clues. The dream rubs ink on its own rules, secret codes and its countenance, obscuring everything as it retreats. These lines merely hint that the dream came but left in disappointment because you were then sleeping with someone, there was a head resting on your arm. This sleep becomes a disgrace to true sleep. Then, there remains only an absurd series of topsy-turvy scenes. Now another part of your body sees a fake dream, delivering false impression and news about you. Your head pressed against the pillow at an uncomfortable angle, the twisted big toe of your left foot and a day-long stomach disorder aggravate the absurdity. The bones of your head retain no traces of authentic dreams. But when you sleep alone in the dark, and it is midnight, the dream grips your body and soul, unlocking its mysteries unto you. The dream leaves you abundantly enriched. When you are alone in a state of powerlessness and helplessness, the dream speaks to you, urging you to inform God that your head is bleeding, for it has received a heavy blow.

As the days rolled by, dreams ceased to visit me. Despite consuming numerous pills, I could snatch little sleep with great difficulty. I felt fidgety and restless all the time. I was turning hollow and desiccated from inside. Neither sorrow nor joy was able to touch me.

To me, people shuffling through their paths resembled still walls. It seemed as if time, surging ahead in the frame of a film before, had suddenly come to a halt. My memory began to fade – even the names of everyday household objects started eluding me. My recollections of my romantic encounters and physical relationships with women also started growing faint. In the end, only she remained – the woman with pale yellow hands and vacant eyes. She loved me deeply, not for my animal passion and vigour alone. It is only she the strand of whose blue scarf I always carry in my mouth. I owe her a great deal for revealing to me the transitory nature of the soul. She showed me the album of my sins. She familiarised me with the purity and charm of my sins. She wasn't my lawfully wedded wife. She did not belong to my religion either. But she always kept the Karva Chauth fast for me. She adorned her hands with the paste of mehndi leaves, wore red bangles in her pale yellow hands and adorned her forehead with a large red bindiya. All these exuded beauty and purity, evoking a deep sense of pity in me. Her body remained famished and parched just to indulge the soul to satiety. It offered a few crumbs of biscuits made of refined flour in order to appease the soul, and the soul devoured them ravenously like a dog. Yes, indeed, like a dog. The body adorned itself tastefully, and the soul felt gratified. Alas! This shameless, cheap soul, none of its miniscule particle enjoys immortality. Won't this soul have derived great pleasure from the jingling of bangles caused by the trembling of weak, yellow hands, famished and parched from Karva Chauth fasting?

This practice has endured through time immemorial. The poor body presents its blood-filled heart tastefully on a platter to the soul for the sake of its pleasure. However, the soul's lust never reaches satiety. Ironically, the soul feigns seeking refuge in religion – how thankless of the soul!

With multiple gaping wounds on his back and a cracked head, the man has long wandered this mortal world like an illusion. Meanwhile, his body wavers unsteadily, holding a plate adorned with Karva Chauth fasting in the gloomy light of a feeble wick.

She would have continued doing it in this manner indefinitely for centuries if not for her realisation, like mine, of the hollowness of the world. Perhaps she too will have seen the picture inverted. That is why, despite her deep love for me and her desire to live and die for me, she wishes to sever ties with me. The white, sharp-pointed bones are piercing her eyes. And it happened for the first time that a sudden dizzy spell and cold sweat caught me off guard while I was sitting before her. That was the day when I left her house not like a dog but like a shameless pig.

CHAPTER THIRTEEN

I DIDN'T DERIVE ANY PLEASURE FROM MY DEBAUCHERY and misdeeds. To me, lust is more fulfilling than sexual acts, just as silence is more profound than sound and darkness better than light. I drew true joy from my beautiful dreams. Alas! Those dreams stopped after my marriage. Those dreams were never solitary – they were always accompanied by someone or something in the darkness whether a person, an animal, a tree or a bicycle. Those dreams hummed the gay tunes of obscenity like a requiem or dirge. My perverse and insane desire used to be present there with one shadow or another always wrapped around my body to maintain its illusion. However, it all occurred amidst the ruins of an infertile and desolate place. Apparently, my body remained motionless. A thick layer of darkness shrouded it. But within the blood coursing through it, a tumultuous gathering occurred where foul and filthy abuse swayed like a qawwali singer immersed in refrain. Purity and filth were inseparable there, as were the virgins from the debauched, and the eyes from the navel. Those dreams were wholly democratic. They were intertwined like the hidden recesses of the brain. If a finger was gently placed on a recess, blood began to congeal there. I was utterly truthful in those dreams, far from hypocrisy. I deserted none, neither my fear, nor hatred, nor my desire. I didn't brush off any dust in my dreams. Alas! They stopped coming, rendering my life colourless and tasteless. I became withdrawn, retreated into myself. The knife hidden in my side etched lines on every scene before my eyes. I grew weary of the lamentably scratched and scraped scenes of the world. Whatever I ate nauseated me. My liver turned sluggish and started to falter, my face swelled up. Gradually, I got fettered by a chain of nameless and indescribable doubts. Although Suicide had been swinging by my knickers ever since my childhood, these days she had started to walk on my clothes. She began to talk to me. Most of the time, she advised me to slit my own throat with the knife I kept hidden with great caution for killing my father. I developed a peculiar fondness for her company. I felt a sense of security in her presence.

As the summer days drew to a close, a gentle coolness softly set in. It gently pushed the heat aside, much like someone carefully dusting off the arms of a chair. One evening, as I lay in bed, my mind empty and eyes staring at the wall of the room, a nameless, eerie terror enveloped me, sending a chill down my spine. The bright bulb in the room seemed to dim, and the walls appeared scraped clean of all colour and varnish. The noise from the street, filtering in through the window, transformed into mysterious whisperings. Restless and fidgety, I turned on my side and the shadow of my body quaked on the wall in a way that filled me with terror. Detached from my body, the shadow foretold ominous possibilities. I suspected that a mild spasm radiated from my left shoulder to the wrist. I felt the pain creep towards my heart, just as a black snake slithers towards a weak rat crouching in a corner. As if a heavy piece of stone settled on my heart, I found it hard to breathe. For no reason at all, a dog began to let out piteous cries in the street just after dusk.

Suddenly, my wife entered the room after taking a bath. Her clothes were sticking to her wet body. Water was dripping from her untied hair. In that moment, she appeared transformed, a tall and muscular woman. Her short body seemed to have stretched like a rubber and was elongated. She also looked very wide. Her bare arms resembled those of a strong, muscular man – biceps bulged on her arms. There was a strange hardness on her face. Maybe she had turned into a stone that becomes larger from lying in water for a long time. The stone was growing larger. It was getting harder. However, it must surely be melting from within.

Who was this woman? I searched her face for my wife's features, but she seemed like an animal that strays onto a black concrete road from within a grassland. I felt a tremor rumble through my flesh, bones and skin, as if I were on the verge of a cardiac arrest. An overwhelming fatigue gripped me, my hands and legs turned cold. But a strange heat curled up beside my heart, settling in the pores of my chest. I grew dizzy. The walls and floor spun like a hot whirlwind on a desolate afternoon.

Then it spouted – that mysterious cold sweat. It was in this moment that it had tapped my body for the first time. She retreated only after pouring the dense darkness of insight into me. Ever since that day, she has visited me almost every day. My vest is perpetually soaked. This dirty vest reeks of blood.

CHAPTER FOURTEEN

THIS MYSTERIOUS COLD SWEAT UTTERLY TRANSFORMED my sexual life. Even if half-heartedly and without enthusiasm, prior to this incident, I used to successfully make love with my wife daily. It had no fixed routine. When I sensed her desire, I would indulge in a sadistic pleasure like a savage, driven by libido.

But everything changed after that evening. Now, I have discovered the existence of a great impotent within me. The erect male organ seemed to me like a cheap, violent emperor wielding momentary power. This emperor needed a vision so profound that after that it would transform itself into a beggar, renouncing worldly pleasure and disappearing into the dark cave of its existence. And the private part of a woman with orgasm was perhaps the saddest among the things I had ever seen, a dried and silent yellow leaf fallen from a tree. As I gazed at this dry yellow leaf, I would quietly begin to weep. The act of sex had now become a dreadful accident for me. I was a body fallen prey to an epileptic fit, devoid of manners, decency and wisdom. The central issue lay in the dread born from the struggle my unfortunate body underwent when my organ refused to dance to the tune of the flesh. And it would turn rebellious, because it possessed its independent personality and distinct character, complete with veins, blood, face, and even a brain. This face and brain were distinctly different from the man's false face, which is painted and worn with a coat and a neck-tie.

And in such times, a poor man's body, his chest, heart, lungs and the discs of his spine, are engaged in a life-threatening labour, fighting the terror of the moment when the woman lying beneath him has not yet reached her orgasm. This is the deadly moment in which a man demonstrates the power that never resided within him. It's a scene of contradictions, fraught with danger. Preyed upon by nervous spasm, he demonstrates an artificial strength, straining every nerve, holding his breath and gasping for air. His lungs and kidneys feel as if they're about to burst, and his spine seems on the verge of breaking, and as he tastes the blood in his saliva he appears to have brought himself to the brink of death. Has anyone ever truly seen the face of a man dying in such a manner?

I have been competing with this empty world with such a farcical power – the power that a man demonstrates when the woman lying under him seethes with arousal. But his organ behaves abruptly, like an alien animal, an unruly, errant horse that throws its rider off and gallops a short distance away to graze indifferently on the grass of its choice. What else can be cited as a rare and greater example of braving hardship in this world and confronting this world's challenges? This was the great impotence that I had so intensely felt in me. Those days I was perpetually gripped by the dizzy spell, cold sweat and anxiety – no doubt I was also enriched by them. They not only afforded me insight and enlightenment but also meted out punishment for my sins like a stern disciplinarian and hard taskmaster. I had sins both within and outside me. Lingering in my pores my sins were covered with sweat. And the place where I sat was a bundle of dry woods of my sinfulness. The patch of Earth covered by this bundle would never yield flowers, because the land where flowers bloom is not a piece of actual land on Earth. We never set our foot on the real Earth. The real piece of Earth is suspended in the air, propping against unknown planks and bamboos. My conscience smites me, denouncing and cursing my body. Why doesn't my conscience understand the simple fact that even a dog can slip sometimes on a banana peel. The glistening beads of cold sweat and the spells of dizziness afford me opportunities to see through the pathetic and ridiculous emptiness of the world we live in. I have already seen the pictures hanging from the walls made of vile smoke. I have also witnessed the absurd spectacle of people madly throwing daggers at them.

Those were the days when Suicide, my inseparable shadow, had turned more talkative. She whispered various things in my ears, even made futile attempts to sing me a lullaby. She made me acutely aware of my depression, repeatedly drawing my attention to an old, rusty axe in a corner of the house with which I could rid myself of this disgraceful and foul head. I constantly ignored Suicide's murmurings. But at the same time I grew increasingly fond of her. Whenever she left me alone and went off for a brief period, or hid herself, I felt her absence intensely. I would be lonely and miserable in her absence. Absolutely helpless.

CHAPTER FIFTEEN

LIKE AN EXPERIENCED TEACHER, SUICIDE BEGAN TO painstakingly caution me against the foolishness and injurious effects of staying within the confines of body. She meticulously enumerated every flaw and underlying defect in the body.

I was gripped by a terrible cold and cough. My nose constantly dripped with dirty, yellow mucus. The cold began to tell on my nerves. My heart shivered. There was no warmth anywhere. Heat emanated only from violent bouts of coughing. The warm air from the fever caused by the cold escaped from my mouth, and my breath floated in my lungs in a way that made me imagine I was running in a field. It felt like I had a wound on my depression-afflicted head. The wound was half-dried and half-healed. A half-dried wound on the body is always dangerous and mysterious. This dried layer is like a swear word heard in dreams, like the humiliations endured in dreams; it is like the names heard in dreams, which are laughed away and forgotten on waking up. But perhaps the names heard in a man's dreams wait until the last edge of his life, where they catch hold of his hand and transform even him into a name heard in a dream. I have always missed my mother with great intensity. I had fallen into the clutches of diseases, become weak and was losing weight. I wanted to suckle my mother.

'Come on, buddy, come out of the confines of the body,' Suicide leaned forward to say in my ear. But I turned a deaf ear to her whispering.

A severe cramp persisted in my stomach. I would feel the urge to go to the toilet after just a gulp of water going down the throat. Then, most of my time was spent sitting over the pot. It was the same toilet from my childhood. It had undergone no change. Narrow and dark, with a decrepit door, a rusty pipe and an old tap with a spout jug beneath it. The aluminium jug had holes in its bottom. The water dripping from the holes would keep the discoloured cemented floor perpetually wet. There was a small niche in the wall where a candle would always be kept. The smoke of the candle had turned the niche black. I would keep squatting on the ugly, dirty yellow seat crawling with cockroaches and ants. I had a very old relationship with this place. After all, it was here that I first heard the crying voice from the rusty, dripping pipe at the age of five.

One day as I sat there, my eyes suddenly fell on the toilet seat. It felt as if my wife had painted the seat in places with her lipstick. The wind blowing outside shook the doors mildly. Dusk had fallen and it was getting dark outside. I lit the candle kept in the niche and peered at the lipstick marks on the toilet seat. No, it wasn't lipstick. It was thick blood sticking to certain spots on the white and yellow seat. My legs shivered terribly. The blood had come from my intestines. It had been formed from my tears that had seeped into my intestine instead of welling up in my eyes when I was five years old.

'Come on, buddy. Come out of your worthless, foul body.' This time Suicide was louder, more assertive. Instantly, my hand holding the burning candle darted to set fire to my clothes. But then the thought of the knife in my safekeeping flashed through my mind. First, I should kill my father.

Was this the meaning of living inside one's body?

I stopped caring about the body. I became unkempt, dirty and filthy. My skin turned ashen brown. My nails, filled with dirt, grew as long as two inches, and I started drawing scratches on my body with them. I began nicking my fingers at their joints with my pale, worm-infested teeth. The fingers developed ugly gaping wounds which knew no healing. I started urinating on those wounds. Since my body, both from the inside and outside, were grimly filthy now, dipping the finger in urine or in blood pumping through the heart felt almost the same.

The number of ants in the toilet began to multiply. The stream of my urine became thicker and whiter. It had traces of sugar. My bones were dissolving and the eyesight was getting weaker. Was this what it meant to stay within the confines of the body? I was plagued by various doubts and suspicions. I stopped shaving my beard, wanting to hide myself and my body from everyone's eyes. I wanted to cover not only my face but my entire body with the growing beard. I was afraid lest my body should reach someone's stomach someday, end up like a tapeworm buried under the faeces and be flushed out with the powerful rush of water into the drain. So I carefully hid my frail body behind a thick beard, filth and foul smell.

The doctors changed my medication. Now I swallowed pills that my father and wife together shoved into my mouth with great difficulty. My house was full of my dirt, phlegm, lice and foul smell.

These were all my sins emerging from my body and falling down around me. How much should I think about my sins? Perhaps the progeny of sin, I search for the ancient relics of my sins. I use my hands like a shovel to dig the ground. My hands get entangled in dangerous roots. I bring these roots close to my eyes and see. My roots are like the form of a woman. Here is the whole spectacle – when my heart desired lust, my brain whimpered. In fact, one more tragedy befell me – I entered human life through the wrong door. Life was a vast mansion with different entrances for different people. The door through which a scavenger entered also happened to be my entrance. I was an untouchable. And just as the whole world becomes untouchable and worthy of hatred for the scavenger, so did it for me. After all, why weren't my roots shaped like a horse or a rabbit? It was simply a matter of forming knots, a simple twist or bend, but that didn't happen. The sound of sin was embedded in my first mournful cries. My sins were the burnt ashes with which I rubbed the utensils of my body clean.

Now this body had become a loathsome object, a thing of disdain. And Suicide persistently advised me to break free by tearing down its wall. I will think about it at leisure. Right now, I have no respite from the relentless scrutiny of my sins. I defer everything to some later time. Once again, I find myself reflecting on my sins which will surely be recorded in my personal book of death rather than in God's book of death.

My worst sin was that I pronounced 'love' like 'sin'. The shattered splinters of my heart cling to the bright line of sin like ants. My sorrowful heart is licking and devouring these sins as termites consume a house, or as dysentery ravages your intestines. My blue shirt of sorrow is drenched with the sweat of hard labour born from the sins. It leaves its colour on my back, a blue stain resembling ink. A map of the hidden treasure of inner wounds and sorrows has been tattooed on my back forever with this blue sweat. It can't be rubbed clean. It is the destiny of my nasty and tainted back. There were tears once that could cleanse these blue marks. Unfortunately, they rolled down the eyes and halted on the chest. Those tears were not as tall as I am. They did not reach my back – where are the eyes on the back? The letters of that unknown and lost language, the language of the body and trauma, were inscribed on my back where the entire map lay hidden. My eyes neither saw it nor cleansed it. Only my spine felt its cold presence. I know well that the day will come when all hatred, infidelities, delinquencies, complaints and kicks will get buried under the cool sand of sin. They will sing a dirge on the inevitable annihilation of this lamentably empty world, mimicking the sound of revelry and celebration and the rhythm of an old drum. Both the celebration and the drum will trample and crush the old sins, reducing them to shreds. And with the same sand, they will form a rich and fertile soil for new generations to sow their sins in. But I – a bastard child, a progeny of sin, carrying a head with depression from a terrible blow – will wander aimlessly, a knife tucked into the waistband of my pyjamas. This is the very knife with which I must kill my father. I have now taken a pledge to fulfil this task and have already made all the necessary preparations. On one pan of the balance scale, I have placed the life I've lived and the time that has passed; on the other pan, there is the weight of my father's murder. It is true that these measuring weights are soiled and disgusting, covered in dust. They are filthy and obscene, and their numbers have long since been rubbed out. Surely, these measuring weights are unreliable. They weigh much less than my destiny or life, which began within the womb of my mother. But justice is to be delivered with these weights. Though it amounts to dishonesty. And who knows when the powerful, invisible hand of honesty will hold me accountable for the crime of keeping these measuring weights of murder, dispatching me to hell. But now it is done. I have placed those black weights on one pan of the balance scale, and on the other one, I have seated myself.

CHAPTER SIXTEEN

DAYS OF INTENSE COLD ARE APPROACHING. THE distance between wound and pus is continually reducing. Soon, I will walk inside a wound as tall as a full-grown man, filled with pus and blood, and wriggling like a worm. Yes, it will give off a fetid smell, but still it'll be a new stench. After all, how long can I bear the burden of this bier? Its weight has left my shoulders rotten. The stench comes from there too, and a wetness seeps into my armpits. The left shoulder gets dislocated repeatedly. That's why it is good that the distance between the wound and pus is disappearing. I have spent all day sharpening the blade of my knife. Several days have passed without my breaking out in cold sweat, without my feeling light-headed. The path of intuition has been blocked by vile and malevolent medicines. Suicide has become reticent. But she sits on my shoulder constantly, like a crow perched on the back of a buffalo grazing in a meadow.

I feel as though I have entered a cold rubber balloon and seated myself inside it. The cold balloon rises up slowly. And I rise with it, higher and higher. I enter a towering, white cloud made of frozen snow. My memory falters now, unable to remember anything. It is as if someone has drained all the blood from my brain. Am I losing consciousness? No, I am regaining it. I am coming back from a long walk in my sleep. My wife and father have bound my hands and feet and have shovelled numerous blue pills into my mouth. These are the same pills in whose haze I passed a large part of my life. I kept walking in sleep, receiving kicks while slumbering. The blasts of sleep escaping from my mouth and head dissolved into my slippers lying on the floor. Paralyzed by sleep, my body was tied up, sometimes in the toilet and sometimes on the remote, dilapidated platform of the house, using the same ropes that once tethered the dogs. In sleep, I ate food from the same utensils used to feed the dogs, and chewed all the bones lying in the gravy. I also saw in my sleep the woman with pale yellow hands crying. I also heard her abusing me, her swear words directed at my mother. I scrubbed away those shameful swear words directed at my mother just as I would clean a utensil. How long should I go on scrubbing this utensil clean? My ancient soul clings to the shameful utensil of grief like a rotting roti stuck to a pot.

There was nothing but endless sleep. In my deep slumber, I saw God and Satan fighting in their respective lights, arguing and debating, then dissolving into laughter during dark nights filled with palpable silence, and joining together seriously to write the book of death in black letters. No decision could be made. Overtaken by deep sleep, I could not discern whether the devil played tricks, or if it was God who devised a plan against him.

After continuing for a long time, for what seems like thousands of centuries in sleep, now I also realise that I constantly headed forward, though leaving a dirty, muddy path behind me. Wherever I passed, a filthy drain formed. When I return, the leeches of that drain will suck all the blood from my calves. My dark shadow-like body will be forced to dive into black and murky swamps. The leaves of the lotus will rot inside the marshy land. The fever gripping my body churns in its own whirlpool, giving the mud the breath and width of a vast river. I will become bespattered with this mossy, mud-filled water, and all the menacing bushes and brambles, the product of my own unconsciousness and sleep, will cling to my head, belly and back. The journey back will not be easy.

But I am coming back. I can clearly see that black trail left by my hapless feet, the black liquid spilling from my desolate toes and unlucky heels.

With all my strength in my lungs and throat, I have expelled the lingering sleep from my body exactly like one forcefully spits out after clearing their throat and saying, *Aakh thoo*. The wild energy within me feels pleasant now. Now I have no fear, no worry and no regard for anything. I have squashed all those leeches with my powerful hands. I have blown all the bushes and brambles far away from me with a blast of my feverish breath. I am filled with overwhelming rage and fury. I am in search of a lion on whose jaw I want to land a heavy punch knocking out all its teeth. Infuriated, I am roaming around with the entire universe on my finger like a paper globe. Moreover, I do not allow this vile and insignificant Suicide to sit even on my nose like a fly. The shameless creature is circling around me, buzzing. Who listens to such droning under these conditions?

I am coming back, lifting the mountain on my palms, kicking the ground like the most powerful man of my time. The Earth quakes violently beneath my feet. My strength is making me a stranger to myself. To alienate and become stranger to myself, I speak continuously. I have turned into a constant murmur of voices. The words spilling from my mouth represent the sound of an advancing fire, threatening to burn everything to ashes. An immense glossary of words pours out of my throat like flaming fire. I speak tirelessly, relentlessly.

My hand is holding that open knife, its blade dazzling. I have kicked my father, sending him sprawling to the ground. I climb on top of him, my knees planted firmly on his chest. My father's grizzled beard quivers pitiably, and his eyes are wide with terror. I grip the knife tightly in my demonic hand, lifting it high above in the sky, so that the knife can pierce my father's chest with a single jab. I don't know from where, but a huge crowd gathers. They catch hold of me. My father survives but he lies on the ground, wriggling helplessly and rubbing his heels like a dying man. But it makes no difference to me. I will repeat my attack, my knife will open again with a petrifying clatter.

To me, it feels as if days and nights are ceasing. How much time has passed in this state of oblivion and immense ecstasy, I don't remember. All I remember is that I am born truly alive for the first time.

Despite the piercing cold, I have started to feel an intense heat rising from within me. My entire body has turned into a boiling cauldron, with my bones simmering in it. Smallpox blisters filled with pus have erupted all over my body. I have torn off my clothes and thrown them away, feeling no shame. The shameless ones are this world, my father, my wife, the woman with pale yellow hands and a crow perched on the electric wires. I roam about naked, urinating into their mouths. I have already launched hundreds of murderous assaults on my father. My knife has left numerous cuts and scratches on his face. Tears trickle down his eyes, aggravating the hot sting of those cuts and scratches. My father lets out desperate cries and flees from me in mortal fear. But I surge like a horrible deluge. I trample all over the soil that crushed me once. I bend over the turbid water of a pond to look at my face. It is the face of a lion with a majestic mane. I feel a strong desire for intimacy. I want to make love with a lioness. My wife and the women around me seem like trivial female-mice scurrying on the ground. I want to crush them under my heavy foot until they are reduced to a pulp, then grab them by their plait-like tails and fling them far into the drain. A demon has taken occupation of my belly, and my hunger knows no satiety. I crave to gobble up and devour something every moment. I gorge myself on countless rotis and pieces of meat, chewing small bones and sucking the large ones. My house and streets are piled high with the bones I have sucked and discarded. I eat constantly, everywhere, while lying on the ground, while sitting in the toilet. I want to wolf down everything including the humans, animals, trees and even walls and roads. I want to rip everything to shreds with my lion-like mouth and fill my insatiable stomach. I kill countless chameleons in cold blood. They drop down from the trees, making tapping sounds. I crush them with my feet, one by one – with each strike, the flow of blood increases in torrents in my body. Now I spoil the lush green fields of sesame, relentlessly rolling off the high piles of sesame seeds and kicking them hard. My naked body is covered with the seeds. I am a raging flood of black water, surging forward. I will wash away everything through my flood. The utensils of the dogs' feed, their collars, ropes, electric poles and my father's corpse will all float in the deluge.

The foundations of the houses will tremble, shattering into pieces under the force of the roaring waters. Now, with my frightening black water, I bend over the alleys and sewers. I fall down, my naked body rolling off these drains, as if being bombarded with relentless kicks. But I know that these wound-scars on my body dripping with blood are testaments to my bravery and boldness. These punches and injuries have been inflicted on me by my own powerful hands and elephant-like feet. My anger is aggravating. I have reached the height of frenzy. I want no one to come between me and my way, no one to come behind me, no ant to pursue me and no bird to chirp over my head. But now, children from the street, holding cobbled-stones and bricks, follow me in droves, kicking up a racket. I am not able to sleep. I have reached the parapet of the dry well where this street terminates in a dead end and seated myself over it. Peering into the well, I call out loudly to the girl clad in the white shalwar and that white cat which the people of the neighbourhood had beaten to a pulp and thrown into it. It is a pity that this well is now clogged with garbage. I am not able to sleep – my sleep is frightened of my fury and rage. I approach the stray dogs sprawled by the roadside and lie down beside them. I'm hoping their sleep will enter my body. Even there, the children's stones land near me. The dogs growl and bare their teeth at me, ready to tear me apart. In a fit of rage, I catch hold of one of the dogs by its leg and rip it apart mercilessly, like a predatory animal.

I have recognised it. This is the same dog that had been tied under the tiled roof of a dilapidated house one dark rainy night. Dripping wet in the water flowing off the tiled roof, it had had fits of shivers intermittently. That night, it had sniffed at the blood-soaked shalwar and the torn pieces of the flesh of that innocent girl writhing in agonising pain in the muddy courtyard, the rain lashing against her body. The dog had pounced on her like a predatory animal attacking its prey.

Today, I rip the dog apart and throw it away.

The children follow me in droves, holding cobbled-stones in their hands. I despise these pests. It is all their handiwork. They know nothing except being born and creating disturbances, spoiling pleasure. I will land on their heads severe blows, so they suffer from depression. To hell with the children, to hell with the women, to hell with this world … I rush into my house and lift the drum, which has lain silently under dust in the junk room for years. I begin to beat it loudly. I hang the drum around my naked body. I beat it as I wander from one street to another. I think of no one, just my mother. I want to go back into her womb again. I relentlessly beat the drum on the roads and then roll off into the drains. I begin to sing in a deep state of unconsciousness. I am not playing any tune. I have turned myself into a tune.

There's no one who won't hear my boisterous song, is there?

I barge into a butcher shop and bash my head against the bare bones lying there; blood gushes out of it profusely. But the bones can't inflict any real harm. I toss pieces of raw meat into the sky to feed the kites and the crows. Looking upwards, I shout, 'Oh kites with eggs and fledglings, come on. Oh kites with eggs and fledglings, come on. No, I am not calling anyone for help. I am just challenging this empty world.' I shout like an enraged elephant so that this hollow world can come and join me in this symphony. This meaningless world must call out to the kites and the crows in the sky because if there was ever a Creator of this world, He has now gone somewhere else after kicking its head away. He is busy arguing and fighting with the devil over the copyright to the book of death.

The children have relentlessly pelted me with stones. Inflicted with wounds my body droops. I perpetually spit on the road, turning the black road of coal tar white. I sink my teeth into the back of every passer-by. I am aware of a rotting tooth in my jaw, but I cling to it like a worm clings to an elephantine yet decaying tooth. I slowly fill it with venom until it turns completely black and hollow.

I don't know how long it has been since I last ate. Like a beggar on the street, I stretch out both hands, asking for a roti. I am famished and racked by hunger pangs. I see thousands of children approach me from one side, clutching stones. From the other side, the people of my street emerge in droves, advancing with spiteful intentions. In this chaos, I spot my father at the forefront, and I start fumbling for my knife on my naked body. I want to pull out the old knife hidden under my skin, but I can't trace it. Disheartened, I wipe the sleep from my eyes with the pads of my fingers and look up at the sky. It is overcast by a pale yellow haze and countless kites are flying in it.

Pickets line both sides of the street, and even the limitless expanse of the sky seems blocked. Swishing ropes and clanking chains are darting towards me like shadows.

They join together and besiege me. It feels as if the entire world is bawling at a lion with the majestic mane.

Trickling down from both my eyes, my blood gets absorbed into my beard. Far away, the sun has perhaps set. It seems like dusk. Trapped in a cage, I roar, hitting my head on its iron bars.

CHAPTER SEVENTEEN

WHEELS HAVE BEEN ATTACHED TO THE CAGE NOW. Leaving behind the racket of children, the cage, on its wheels, has emerged from the narrow alleys onto the wide open roads. It has traversed a road far from the city. Just a little while ago, the cage passed by the white house in which the woman with pale yellow hands lives. I recognised her voice cursing and abusing me, just like a dog recognises the footsteps of its owner from afar. She was hurling abuses at me, directing her swear words at my mother! '*Haraami*, the one who committed evil deeds with his mother.' The woman who once considered my leftovers a blessing, ate from my plate and said prayers for my safety now cursed me out. Love ... ? With a handkerchief on its nose, love has fled from me. I saw with my own eyes as she stood on her rooftop and threw towards me a white, pointed bone with full force.

The cage now reaches a dirt road. It jerks and bumps along it. I fall repeatedly on the wobbly iron floor from these jolts. Each time, I get up again. My father forcefully opens my closed fist and snatches away all the peanuts.

My mother fights with my father while beating the drum. The area around me begins to plunge into a blackout. The ragged and cold military uniform has been dropped down from a dark window. The darkness is shattered by gunfire. The cage reaches the border of the city near the mounds of the earth behind which lie graves of the wild and unclaimed captives. I catch sight of my mother on one of the mounds. She disappears, then reappears, then recedes. My mother shrinks to a dot, moving further and further away until she slowly disappears completely.

The cage stops near a menacing black wall. Desolation sprawls far into the distance. Ghostly shadows of dense trees sway in their own breeze. I feel like a dreadful jerk. Once again, I have been pushed into the abyss of that terrifying sleep. I have fallen asleep holding the black cage bars in my hand.

CHAPTER EIGHTEEN

IF THERE IS ANY ISSUE REMAINING, IT'S THE ELECTRIC current. I find myself seated perhaps in the executioner's chair with all four limbs bound. My head and ears are covered with a blemished and ugly hood. This is my death sentence that was recorded in the book of death many lifetimes ago. My name has been read in the book of death through a microscope. It is a name crafted by the continuously flowing essence of actions over which I had no control. All my actions and sins were in my pursuit even before my birth.

So today is the day for the judgement to be executed. My destiny is now to be burnt to a cinder in this chair. What difference did it make whether the electric current travelled in a straight line to the executioner's chair or snaked its way up, forming equal lines up and down, creating curls? Whether it was hydroelectricity or the power generated from coal, tides or wind. Though I wished it would have been generated by wind.

These shocks are very severe. I scream loudly, but a wide plastic strap tied across my lips blocks my screams. With each shock, my intestines convulse as if rising to my throat. My urine lets out involuntarily. I am caught in seismic waves. My bones feel as if they are leaving their places, separating from each other. My eyes pop out of their sockets. These shocks do not end. My soul cannot bear the torment of these shocks any longer – it wants to escape, run away, leaving my body tied in this chair. My soul now craves escape.

I don't know if I am alive or dead. But I am no longer in the chair. The electric shocks no longer flow through my body. Perhaps my father has released me from the electric pole in the neighbourhood street. I am lying in a narrow, dark cell like a sick and physically depleted animal, my tongue lolling out. In a corner, there are a few rotis and some lentils or curry in a bowl but I cannot take a bite. Hunger and food are no longer for me.

I don't know how much time has passed. At times, daylight stretches before me for ages, and at times everything remains plunged into darkness. The dawning of day and the falling of night hold no meaning for me. But sometimes, I have an ominous feeling that my old age has arrived within these high black walls. I am addicted to sitting in the executioner's chair every day, relentlessly confronting death sentences. I have grown accustomed to these electric shocks. I no longer writhe in agony, letting out screams. My blood has become used to this poison in the way that a long-term user's blood gets accustomed to drugs. These electric shocks have sucked out all the heat from my blood. The blood coursing through my veins has changed. Like a squeezed out towel, my heart hangs alone from a clothesline, slowly trembling and stirring in the wind. This is a terrifying place. This building, sprawling across miles, is enclosed by black, high and menacing ramparts. The edges of the ramparts are overgrown with weeds. Beyond the walls must be a road from where unceasing roars of passing trucks and lorries keep coming. These sounds become eerily long during the night, creeping me out, inducing fear. Eucalyptus trees, standing in a row with their heads held high, keep peeping over the ramparts. Monkeys jump from the ramparts to the trees and from the trees to the ramparts all day long. And at night, stray cats sit on them and wail.

Long, eerie corridors appear into sight all around this forlorn and cursed building. These murky corridors are the dwellings of ghosts and witches that resemble human beings. Sometimes, they all come together to scream and weep loudly without any reason, and sometimes they burst out laughing, rending the sky asunder. Then, there are times when these narrow, dark cells and corridors, covered with seepage, fall silent like a graveyard. The shadows of their inhabitants visible in the stray lights get jumbled up, and the petrifying figures begin to sway on the walls. These eerie and dangerous galleries often echo with the sound of unseen footsteps. There are some people here who continue to watch over and guard these ghosts day and night. At a short distance, there is a row of small, discoloured and decrepit quarters. One can often see the flickering light of a dim lamp and hear the jarring sound of a burning stove emanating from here. This gloomy sound deepens the silence. In the middle of the night, hyenas are heard roaring with laughter in the distance, and somewhere an owl also hoots, speaking its mysterious and deadly language. But then all these sounds are drowned out by the terrifying rumble of trucks plying on the deserted road outside. Sometimes, heaps of thin rotis and buckets filled with runny, pale yellow dal pile up in these alleys. At times, the inhabitants of these corridors fall on them, throwing rotis and dal at each other, while at other times they don't even bother to look at them.

Almost every day, these human-like ghosts are stripped naked and mercilessly beaten with whips, their heads crushed under kicks.

No one comes from the other side of the wall to visit or speak to them. Those who enter these filthy and dark cells come only to thrash them. In the middle of the beating, the ghosts taking the beating dissolve into loud laughter. Trampled, their bodies roll on the ground, unrestrained peals of laughter erupting from them, then fall silent like dead bodies wrapped in shrouds. These dead bodies stick their heads in the latrines constructed beneath the black walls, and then strain to peer outside. All they see from there are the old trunks of the trees, or perhaps the black rolling wheels of the trucks.

The ghosts inside these ramparts are all my companions, my friends. Despite being strangers to me, they are like me. I have come to believe that, sooner or later, everyone inevitably ends up finding and joining the people who are just like them. What is destined eventually comes to pass. Here, everyone's suicide is clenched in their fist. They walk with their inseparable shadows, often following these shadows towards that fatal direction. They climb those black walls and jump into the embrace of death. No one comes to claim their bodies – no crows or vultures either. They vanish without any trace from every scene along with their suicide. In those moments, Suicide, resting in my torn pocket, looks at me with victorious eyes. Unable to endure the challenges of her gaze, I advance and silently sit down in the executioner's chair. Sitting in this chair earlier, I have admitted my guilt. It is the chair of my confessions. Now I am going inside the executioner's whip, winding my way to receive the punishment for my sins. After the electric shocks, I feel sleepy. This sleep is not the one that is born within my body. It has invaded from the outside. This is a humiliating and vile injection of unconsciousness, or a malicious and filthy handkerchief soaked in chloroform.

Now I get up from the silent chair, lurching to my feet and staggering towards my cell. A heavy rusty box of sleep weighs on my head – the nails on its bottom pierce the part of my head where my memory is buried. I urinate in my sleep. The urine passed in sleep is just like the urine passed in a dream. Along with this urine, the foul odour of sleep also spreads across the dark floor. My dreams have always been like this – they have passed mostly through the footrests of latrines in desolate houses.

After enduring the electric shocks in successive frequency, I have become completely silent these days. The seed of silence, which lay buried within me for ages, has now grown into a dense tree. I feel as if I have touched the soil of an alien planet and come back. Therefore, I have turned mute. My tongue has completely dried up and I cannot even moisten my parched lips. My jaws, palate and throat have frozen. No word escapes from here, no sound is produced, not even the sound of clearing my throat. A horrifying silence has settled in my intestines, chest and throat. But this silence is revealing its secrets to me. It is like a musical piece written on a sheet of paper. What is the meaning of the music written on the sheet of paper? It should have left my head and soared into the air, or it should have leaked into the underworld through the sole of my shoes. But this silent symphony, written on a sheet of paper, has pasted my memory's false face on my back. I feel like lumps of soil eroding from a distant, inhabited island are falling on my back. I feel it clearly today that perhaps, after the entire lifetime has passed, my submerged island is slowly resurfacing. I am experiencing a sleep that is very old, a sleep like that of children. I am frightened. I have covered my face with a filthy, damp sheet. Gripped by irrepressible sleep, I have lost control and fallen on the floor. I am sleeping. Some light penetrates my eyes. There is a wall, and in the wall, there is a rift. From the rift comes a dirty, faint light that is produced by burning garbage. It seems that the sun is going to be eclipsed in the distant sky. In every light, there is a black shadow present. But the part of the sun unaffected by the solar eclipse is more dangerous than the gloomy, eclipsed part of it. If a person happens to see this half-bright sun with his naked eyes, he will turn blind because in his eye comes that black shadow and sits there for ever. This black shadow is equal to the exact portion of the sun where the eclipse does not occur. I can clearly see this black shadow in my bright eyes. There is someone beneath the Earth, like lonely still water – he is approaching me.

My father is forcibly dragging my mother towards the bed. No, no, no more of it now! My mother's voice quivers with terror, but my father has thrown her on the bed.

'No, don't do this. It can't be done now.' My mother's trembling voice is heard. But my father bends over her like the shadow of a dagger as long as a man's height.

The dagger cruelly rips her clothes and leaves her in a state of undress. My mother's belly is swollen in a very pure and sacred way. She looks plump and round from everywhere. There is no trace of any bones in her body. The fragrance of milk emanates from her round and beautiful body.

'No. For God's sake, think about your child. I am in the eighth month of my pregnancy. This is a sin, a sin, a sin.' As if my mother's muffled voice is heard from under heavy debris.

In the compassionate and tranquil darkness around me, a mysterious turmoil is stirred. A patch of darkness near my head gets caught in seismic waves. Darkness begins to shake horribly, unmooring itself from its foundation. I am confronted with an incomprehensible restlessness. Who am I? Where am I? Somewhere between non-existence and the universe, I feel a piercing surge in the flow of my consciousness much before my birth. My dormant five senses are awakened by pain. In this trembling darkness, I sense the stench of rotten fish on my head. I feel nauseated. I feel as if I am wrapped in a silent shroud of snow.

And then suddenly, a heavy blow strikes my weak head. In unbearable pain I start crying uncontrollably. My head is spattered with mud, blood and semen. The stench and the intensity of this pain have stupefied me. I feel giddy but I can't even stir due the shock of the blow. I can't even cry. I am not able to cry. I am on the verge of losing my consciousness. I am dying, no, I am right here, trying to gather my senses at this same blind space. I discover Suicide, my inseparable shadow, from this wall of darkness. And I embrace her and embed her in my consciousness. Now I really want to die. I want to breathe my last in the paradise of darkness. I am sweating profusely, bespattered with blood. The smell of blood has merged into every drop of my sweat. I am abandoning the will to live. I want to let go of the centuries-old desire that brought me to this darkness. But now I don't want to go out of it. I want to return to nothingness. A black shadow creeps into my eye and settles there. I have handed over my life story to both God and Satan to include in the book of death.

CHAPTER NINETEEN

WIPING THE SLEEP TAINTED BY LIGHT FROM MY EYES, I have removed the sheet from my body. The day has dawned but a light rain is falling. Spitting out the remnants of sleep gripping my body, I stand up. The guards of the corridors and cells have come to me. Their inhuman faces are wreathed in smiles – strange smiles which I have never seen before. They speak to me in a language that perhaps I have heard after centuries. They inform me in a threatening tone that my father died last night. Now, they command me to follow them, and I walk behind the executioner. Am I being led to the noose of the swinging gallows? Their heavy boots march ahead of me. I stayed awake all night long. And just when I was about to snatch some sleep, the time for departure arrived. Once again, I am walking against the morning sleep. With my numb and paralysed hands and feet, I am writing a narrative against sleep. Today, all the confessions and eyewitness testimonies have been completed.

But no, they are heading towards the main gate. They bring me the good news that I am now completely free. They have come to the main gate to bid me goodbye. I turn back to glance over those dark alleys and cells, but I cannot see them clearly through the mist of rain. The wild peals of laughter reverberating through that place has ceased. The witches and the ghosts gaze at me fixedly with their blank, gloomy eyes. I feel embarrassed. I cannot face their eyes. I turn my back on them. I am leaving my people, friends and brothers behind. I walk out of this building through a wide, long door, leaving them wandering in those dark corridors, seeking their submerged islands amidst the swish of whips and the loud hissing of the burning stoves. A drenched monkey jumps from the edge of the black wall and suddenly appears before me, staring at me with its bloodshot eyes. I am outside the door, on the road. No one has come to receive me, nor have I been handed over to anyone. I have been entrusted to myself. But she comes running to me, an eight or nine-year-old girl, from inside the building. Her frock is bespattered with mud. The guards push her back inside. But she has come to say goodbye to me. She has broken through the chain of guards and executioners and kissed me. Her lips resemble flowers burnt to a cinder. Perhaps she called me 'Baba'. I know she is no one to me. She was born from this wounded head of mine. She has lived in my head like a foetus for an unknown length of time. She has grown by drinking the blood of my brain and sucking my bones. Now she has come out like a dream. This dream is imprisoned inside the building from which I have come out.

It is raining. The long, desolate road is thoroughly wet. How has it suddenly turned to evening? It was daytime just a short while ago. But now, the melancholic scene of twilight is apparent even in the rain. In front of me, a crow sits silently on the swinging electric wires, getting drenched. A rain-soaked truck loaded with bamboo and wooden beams zooms past the black and wet road, splashing water. Behind me, the main gate closes with a doleful, heavy sound. I cross the road and move forward. Standing on the other side of the road, I look at the black, rain-drenched rampart, it stretches as far as the eyes can see. The wild weeds grown on it sway gently in the wind.

I have carefully read the board hung on the gate of this solitary and bleak building. It is a classroom, the greatest classroom. I now look at its desolate walls with grateful eyes. This is the only place on this void Earth that has led me to my lost underwater island. It has taken my memory deep down and buried it there. The students of this classroom are the wisest and most enlightened human beings in the world. That is why they wander, laughing and crying in those narrow, sombre rooms and deserted corridors. This classroom has revealed to me the mystery of the book of death, which God and Satan were contending over. Now I have come to know that it was not an issue of copyright. One night when God was sleeping, smiling away in his dreams at the sight of the children who were laughing in their mothers' wombs, Satan quietly changed the meaning of death. In God's book, this changed concept and meaning of death did not exist. Satan had written 'death' in place of another word: 'life'. But the ink of Satan's pen was un-erasable. So, their conflict has continued since eternity. But they speak to each other amicably and show all civil courtesies. However, humans are bound to a long series of misunderstandings and delusions, which constitute this world.

But this classroom is a parallel world, completely different from the worlds created by God and Satan. It is a world inhabited by truly wise human beings. This is not a world where someone discreetly hands a dagger to another person, turning their fate into a never-ending and futile struggle, causing them to spend their entire life throwing daggers at mere pictures. In this realm, all objects and people are just images because they are neither completely real nor unreal. They all depend on each other. They have no absolute, self-sufficient existence of their own.

Therefore, after coming out of those benevolent ramparts, I find myself in a world that is the name of an absurd place inhabited by unconscious human beings. To awaken its dwellers, no message, preaching or slogan is required – just a heavy kick on the womb will serve the purpose.

The rain has thinned into a light drizzle. Darkness has begun to spread. Where will I go now? I don't want to walk those terrifying paths again. I don't want to tread the roads constructed only for the return journey. What should I think about my past? The past is the foolish hope of the dead souls – hope that death snatched away and recorded in its black, hard-bound book. So, I no longer regret that I hummed filth and sins like a song. Was it not enough that at least I was able to hum a song? Every object, every emotion and every human appeared before me in a form. Hatred, love, insults, humiliations, tears, punches or miseries all came together to dance madly under the shade of a dense banyan tree. On the rhythm and beat of lust, obscenity and desire, I came to die but I did not even open the book of death, containing Satan's deceit and conspiracy, and God's indifference. Will Buddha accept my blood spurting from the banyan trunk as an offering?

It is good that new cracks are forming in continents or lands. The lava emerging from within the Earth is now tasked with soon becoming a new ocean, sweeping away another large, insensate and deaf part of the Earth. Such valleys and cracks must meet the Red Sea. At least it will be less wild, foul-smelling and foamy than the sea of lust-filled human blood.

The rain turns torrential. Drenched to the skin in this rain, I have reached the muddy ground in my tattered clothes, swaying and trailing. Water is entering my torn shoes. There is a small pit here – it is filled with water. I choose this wonderful place for myself. From here, I will always be able to see the classroom, those black ramparts, that large, solitary and tall main gate. Sitting in front of a classroom is at least better than sitting in front of a mausoleum or shrine.

Suicide, my shadow, a rare idea unique to me, which I have discovered myself, is with me. Everyone must discover their inseparable shadows and bring them under their control. My shadow is now under my control. It is subordinate to me. I have placed Suicide in my torn shoe, like the final weapon that will obey my command at the right time. I am the master of this inseparable shadow. My shoe is the abode of my shadow.

I squat down in the small pit filled with water, and from there I will keep looking at the greatest classroom all my life. I will not climb out from here. Night has fallen. The rain pitter-patters continuously but I also hear the sound of other waters. This is not rainwater. It is being released from far away, very far away. I know that I will drown. But before that, I will turn into a tree and then dry up, transforming into my roots. Then she will come out from the classroom. My daughter, nurtured in the womb of my brain, will use her hands as a shovel to dig into the soil of this pit. My roots will get enmeshed in her hands. These roots will resemble a mother's womb. In order to enter the womb, my daughter won't need to be indebted to a foul drop of merciless semen. Thus her name will never be recorded in the book of death.

Night is advancing. It will end. Then there will be night again. What else does the empty Earth have to do but revolve? But I will not leave this final abode to go anywhere else. The roar of the waters is getting louder. There is no shade of a tree over my head, but I do not care. The wind has suddenly become very strong. The rain has merged with some other water, turning into a raging storm. The trucks plying on the road have stopped. Perhaps, a flood is coming.

I am in the pit, the water has reached my knees. But I know it cannot rise above my head. It will have to recede. Every tide ebbs, so every flood must eventually recede one day. I pat the soaking-wet Suicide resting in my shoe with my hand and, firmly bracing myself against the stormy rain, I bow my head in the dark water of the pit and squat down.

LAST CHAPTER

Also from ekadā

Also from ekadā

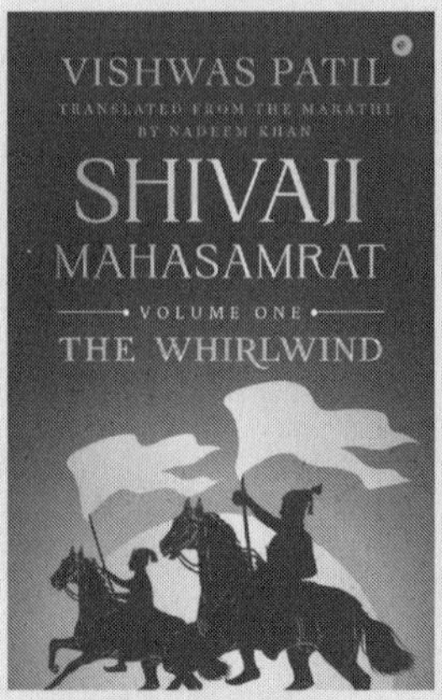

Also from ekadā

Also from ekadā

Also from ekadā

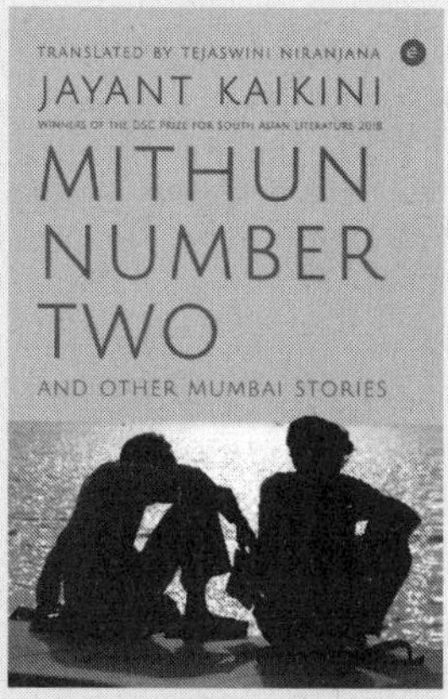

Also from ekadā

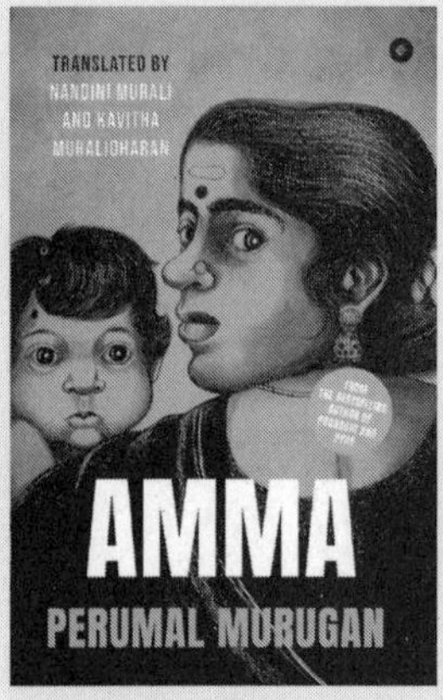

Also from ekadā

Also from ekadā